S. Baring-Gould

Red Spider

Volume 1

S. Baring-Gould

Red Spider
Volume 1

1st Edition | ISBN: 978-3-75235-094-4

Place of Publication: Frankfurt am Main, Germany

Year of Publication: 2020

Outlook Verlag GmbH, Germany.

Reproduction of the original.

RED SPIDER

BY
SABINE BARING-GOULD

VOL. I.

PREFACE.

Fifty years ago! Half a century has passed since the writer was a child in the parish where he has laid the scene of this tale.

There he had a trusty nurse, and a somewhat romantic story was attached to her life. Faithful, good creature! She was carrying the writer in her arms over a brook by a bridge elevated high above the water, when the plank broke. She at once held up her charge over her head, with both arms, and made no attempt to save herself, thinking only of him, as she fell on the stones and into the water. *He* escaped wholly unhurt, owing to her devotion.

Many years after, the author read a little German story which curiously recalled to him his nurse and her career. When a few years ago he revisited the scenes of his childhood, he thought to recall on paper many and many a recollection of village life in the south-west of England in one of its most still and forgotten corners. So he has taken this thread of story, not wholly original in its initiation, and has altered and twisted it to suit his purpose, and has strung on it sundry pictures of what was beginning to fade half a century ago in Devon. Old customs, modes of thought, of speech, quaint sayings, weird superstitions are all disappearing out of the country, utterly and forever.

The labourer is now enfranchised, education is universal, railways have made life circulate freer; and we stand now before a great social dissolving view, from which old things are passing away, and what is coming on we can only partly guess, not wholly distinguish.

In revisiting the parish of Bratton Clovelly, the author found little of the outward scenery changed, but the modes of life were in a state of transition. The same hills, the same dear old moors and woods, the same green coombs, the same flowers, the same old church, and the same glorious landscape. The reader will perhaps accept with leniency a slight tale for the sake of the pictures it presents of what is gone for ever, or is fast fading away. Coryndon's Charity, of course, is non-existent in Bratton parish. The names are all taken, Christian and sire, from the early registers of the parish. Village characteristics, incidents, superstitions have been worked in, from actual recollections. The author has tried to be very close in local colour; and, if it be not too bold a comparison, he would have this little story considered, like one of Birket Foster's water-colours, rather as a transcript from nature than as a finished, original, highly-arranged and considered picture.

CHAPTER I.

THE BROTHERS-IN-LAW.

Heigh! for a badger-skin waistcoat like that of Hillary Nanspian of Chimsworthy! What would not I give to be the owner of such a waistcoat? Many a covetous glance was cast at that waistcoat in the parish church of Bratton Clovelly, in the county of Devon, on Sunday, where it appeared during public worship in a pew; and when the parson read the Decalogue, many a heart was relieved to learn that the prohibition against covetousness did not extend to badger-skin waistcoats. That waistcoat made of the skin of a badger Hillary Nanspian had himself drawn and killed. In colour it was silver-grey graduating to black. The fur was so deep that the hand that grasped it sank into it. The waistcoat was lined with red, and had flaps of fur to double over the breast when the wind lay in the east and the frost was cruel. When the wind was wet and warm, the flaps were turned back, exposing the gay crimson lining, and greatly enhancing its beauty. The waistcoat had been constructed for Hillary Nanspian by his loving wife before she died.

Hillary Nanspian of Chimsworthy was a big, brisk, florid man, with light grey eyes. His face was open, round, hearty, and of the colour of a ribstone pippin. He was, to all appearance, a well-to-do man. But appearances are not always to be trusted. Chimsworthy, where he lived, was a farm of two hundred acres; the subsoil clay, some of the land moor, and more bog; but the moor was a fine place for sheep, and the bog produced pasture for the young stock when the clay grass land was drought-dry. Hillary had an orchard of the best sorts of apples grown in the West, and he had a nursery of apples, of grafts, and of seedlings. When he ate a particularly good apple, he collected the pips for sowing, put them in a paper cornet, and wrote thereon, 'This here apple was a-eated of I on ———,' such and such a day, 'and cruel good he were too.' (*Cruel*, in the West, means no more than 'very.')

The farm of Chimsworthy had come to Nanspian through his wife, who was dead. His brother-in-law was Taverner Langford of Langford. Taverner's mother had been a Hill, Blandina Hill, heiress of Chimsworthy, and it went to her daughter Blandina, who carried it when she married to her Cornish husband, Hillary Nanspian.

Taverner Langford was unmarried, getting on in years, and had no nearer relative than young Hillary Nanspian, his nephew, the only child of his deceased sister Blandina. It was an understood thing in the parish of Bratton Clovelly that young Hillary would be heir to his uncle, and succeed to both Langford and Chimsworthy. Taverner said nothing about this, and took no particular notice of Hillary junior, but, as Hillary senior and the parish argued, if Taverner does not leave everything to the young one, whom can he make his heir? Hillary was a warm-blooded man. He suffered little from cold; he liked to live in his shirt-sleeves. When rain fell, he threw a sack over his shoulders. He drew on his cloth coat only for church and market. He was an imposing man, out of his coat or in it, big in girth, broad in beam, and tall of stature. But especially imposing was he when he rode to market on his white cob, in his badger-skin waistcoat turned up with crimson. The consciousness that he was, or ought to be, a man of substance never left him. His son Hillary would be a wealthy yeoman, and he—he Hillary senior—was the father of this son, this wealthy yeoman prospective. On this thought he puffed himself up. Considering this, he jingled the coins in his pocket. Boasting of this he drank with the farmers till he was as red in face as the lappets of his waistcoat.

Adjoining the house was a good oak wood covering the slope to the brook that flowed in the bottom. Fine sticks of timber had been cut thence, time out of mind. The rafters of the old house, the beams of the cattle-sheds, the posts of the gates, the very rails ('shivers,' as they were locally called), the flooring ('plancheon' locally), all were of oak, hard as iron; and all came out of Chimsworthy wood. An avenue of contorted, stunted limes led to the entrance gates of granite, topped with stone balls; and the gates gave admission to a yard deep in dung. The house was low, part of cob—that is, clay and straw kneaded and unbaked—part of stone laid in clay, not in lime. In the cob walls, plastered white, were oak windows, in the stone walls two granite windows. The house was shaped like the letter T, of which the top stroke represents the stone portion, containing the parlour and the best bedroom over it, and the stairs. The roofs were thatched. There was more roof than wall to Chimsworthy, which cowered almost into the ground.

At the back of the house rose the lofty bank of Broadbury, the highest ridge between Dartmoor and the Atlantic. The rain that fell on the Down above oozed through the shale about Chimsworthy, so that the lane and yards were perpetually wet, and compelled those who lived there to walk in wading boots.

In shape, Broadbury is a crescent, with the horns east and west, and the lap of the half moon lies to the south. In this lap, the nursery of countless streams, stands Chimsworthy, with a bank of pines behind it, and above the black pines golden gorse, and over the golden gorse blue sky and fleecy white clouds. The countless springs issue from emerald patches of bog, where bloom the purple butterwort, the white grass of Parnassus, the yellow asphodel, and the blood-tipped sundew. The rivulets become rills, and swell to brooks which have scooped themselves coombs in the hill slope, and the coombs as they descend deepen into valleys, whose sides are rich with oak coppice, and the bottoms are rank with cotton grass, fleecy and flickering as

6

the white clouds that drift overhead.

Chimsworthy had originally belonged to the Hills, a fine old yeoman family, but the last of the Hills had carried it by marriage to the Langfords of Langford. How it had gone to Hillary Nanspian by his marriage with the daughter of Mrs. Langford has already been told.

Langford had been owned for many generations by the Langfords, once a gentle family, with large estates both in Bratton Clovelly and in Marham Church, near Bude in Cornwall. Nothing now remained to Taverner but the ancestral house and the home estate of some four hundred acres. Chimsworthy had been united with it by his father's marriage, but lost again by his sister's union with the Cornishman Nanspian.

Something like twenty-four months of married life was all that poor Blandina had; and since he had lost his wife, Hillary had remained a widower. Many a farmer's daughter had set her eyes on him, for he was a fine man, but in vain. Hillary Nanspian had now lived at Chimsworthy twenty-two years. His son Hillary was aged twenty.

Langford was a different sort of place from Chimsworthy, and Taverner Langford was a different sort of man from Hillary Nanspian. Langford stood higher than Chimsworthy. It was built on the edge of Broadbury, but slightly under its lea, in a situation commanding an extensive and superb view of Dartmoor, that rose against the eastern horizon, a wall of turquoise in sunshine, of indigo in cloudy weather, with picturesque serrated ridge. The intermediate country was much indented with deep valleys, running north and south, clothed in dark woods, and the effect was that of gazing over a billowy sea at a mountainous coast.

Not a tree, scarce a bush, stood about Langford, which occupied a site too elevated and exposed for the growth of anything but thorns and gorse. The house itself was stiff, slate roofed, and with slate-encased walls, giving it a harsh metallic appearance.

Taverner Langford was a tall, gaunt man, high-shouldered, with a stoop, dark-haired, dark-eyed, and sallow-complexioned. He had high cheekbones and a large hard mouth. His hair was grizzled with age, but his eyes had lost none of their keenness, they bored like bradawls. His eyebrows were very thick and dark, looking more like pieces of black fur glued on to his forehead than natural growths. He never looked any one steadily in the face, but cast furtive glances, with which, however, he saw vastly more than did Hillary with his wide grey-eyed stare.

Taverner Langford had never married. It had never been heard in Bratton that he had courted a girl. His housekeeping was managed by a grey-faced, sour woman, Widow Veale. As Hillary Nanspian was people's churchwarden, Taverner Langford was parson's churchwarden. The Reverend Mr. Robbins, the rector, had appointed him, at the Easter vestry five years before the opening of this tale, because he was a Dissenter. He did this for two reasons: first, to disarm Langford's opposition to the Church; and secondly, to manifest his own tolerance—an easy tolerance that springs out of void of convictions. The two wardens were reappointed annually. They and two others acted as feoffees of an estate left in charity for the poor. They let the land to each other alternate years at a shilling an acre, and consumed the proceeds in a dinner at the 'Ring of Bells' once a year. The poor were provided with the scraps that fell from the feoffees' table.

Taverner Langford was respected in the place and throughout the neighbourhood, because he represented a family as old as the parish church, a family which had once owned large possessions, and maintained some state; also because he was an exceedingly shrewd man, whom no one could overreach, and who was supposed to have amassed much money. But he was not a popular man. He was taciturn, self-contained, and shunned society. He drank water only, never smoked nor swore; with the farmers he was unsociable, with the labourers ungracious, in all his dealings he was grasping and unyielding. Dishonourable he was not; unscrupulous he was not, except only in exacting the last penny of his bargains.

Hillary Nanspian's presence was commanding and he was fond of his glass, smoked and swore; the glass, the pipe, and an oath all links of good fellowship. Nevertheless, he also was not a popular man. In the first place he was a foreigner—that is, a Cornishman; in the second, he was arrogant and boastful.

The brothers-in-law got on better with each other than with others. Each knew and allowed for the other's infirmities. Towards Taverner Hillary bated his pride; he had sufficient discretion not to brag in the presence of a man to whom he owed money. Hillary was a bad man of business, wasteful, liberal, and careless of his money. He had saved nothing out of Chimsworthy, and, after a run of bad seasons, had been forced to borrow of his brother-in-law to meet current expenses.

Taverner and Hillary were not cordial friends, but they were friends. Taverner felt, though he did not acknowledge, his isolation, and he was glad to have his brother-in-law to whom he could open his lips. Knowing himself to be of a good old gentle family, Taverner kept himself from terms of familiarity with the farmers, but he was too close with his money to take his place with the gentry.

There was one point on which Hillary irrationally sensitive; there was also a point on which Taverner was tender. Each avoided touching the delicate and irritable spot in the other. Once, and only once, had Nanspian flared up at a word from Langford, and for a moment their friendship had been threatened with rupture.

Hillary Nanspian was, as has been said, a Cornishman, and the rooted, ineradicable belief of the Devonians is that their Celtic Trans-Tamarian neighbours are born with tails. The people of Bratton Clovelly persisted in asserting that Nanspian had a tail concealed under his garments. When first he entered the parish, rude boys had shouted after inquiries about the caudal appendage, he had retaliated so unmercifully, that their parents had resented it, and the chastisement, instead of driving the prejudice out, had deepened it into indelible conviction. 'For why,' it was argued, 'should he take on so, unless it be true?'

9

He was annoyed at church by the interested attention paid to him by the women and children when he seated himself in the Chimsworthy pew, and when riding to market, by the look of curiosity with which his seat on the saddle was watched by the men.

The only occasion on which the friendship of Langford and Nanspian threatened a cleavage, was when the former, whether with kindly intention or sarcastically cannot be determined, urged on Hillary the advisability of his publicly bathing in the river Thrustle, one hot summer day, so as to afford ocular demonstration to the people of the parish that they laboured under a delusion in asserting the prolongation of his spine. This proposition so irritated Nanspian, that he burst into a tempest of oaths, and for some weeks would not speak to his brother-in-law. Though eventually reconciled, the recollection of the affront was never wholly effaced.

The sensitive point with Taverner Langford was of a very different nature. Not being a married man he was obliged to engage a housekeeper to manage his dairy, his maids, and his domestic affairs generally. His housekeeper, Mrs. Veale, was a vinegary woman, of very unpleasant appearance. She managed admirably, was economical, active, and clean. The mere fact, however, of her being at Langford was enough to give rise to some scandal. She was intensely disliked by all the servants on the farm and by the maids in the house.

'Why don't Mr. Langford get rid of the woman, so ill-favoured, so sharp-tongued, so unpleasant, unless he can't help hisself?' was reasoned. 'You may depend on it there's something.'

Taverner was touchy on this matter. He broke with Farmer Yelland for inquiring of him flippantly, 'How goes the missus?'

Langford detested the woman, who had a livid face, pink eyes, and a rasping voice; but as scandal attached to him with such a creature in his house, he argued: How much more consistency would it assume had he a better favoured housekeeper!

'Moreover,' he reasoned, 'where can I get one who will look after my interests so well as Mrs. Veale? If she be bitter to me, she's sloes and wormwood to the servants.'

CHAPTER II.

THE MONEY-SPINNER.

A little spark will burn a big hole—a very little spark indeed was the occasion of a great blaze of temper, and a great gap in the friendship of the brothers-in-law. Langford possessed this disadvantage: it lay so high, and was so exposed, that it lacked cosiness. It had nowhere about it a nook where a man might sit and enjoy the sun without being cut by the wind. Broadbury was the meeting-place of all the winds. Thither the wind roared without let from the Atlantic, and to the back of it every tree bowed from the north-west; thither it swept from the east with a from the rocky crests of Dartmoor, sparing the intervening park-like lowlands.

Chimsworthy had no prospect from its windows; but it stood at the source of an affluent of the Tamar, and beyond its granite gates, across the lane that led up to Broadbury, was a stile, and beyond the stile a slope with a view down the valley to the setting sun and the purple range of Cornish tors above Liskeard, Caradon, Boarrah, Kilmar, and Trevartha.

On Sunday evenings, and whenever the fancy took him, Taverner Langford would descend Broadbury by the lane, cross the stile, and seat himself on a rude granite slab on the farther side of the hedge, that had been placed there by one of the Hills—it had been the 'quoit' of a great prehistoric dolmen or cromlech, but the supporters had been removed to serve as gateposts, and the covering-stone now formed a seat. On this stone Taverner

Langford spent many an hour with his chin on the handle of his thorn stick, looking over the wood and meadows and arable land of Chimsworthy, and scheming how money might be made out of the farm were it profitably worked. He noted with jealous eye the ravages caused by neglect, the gaps in the hedges, the broken roofs, the crop of thistles, the choked drains bursting many yards above their mouths, bursting because their mouths had not been kept open. The farm had been managed by Taverner's father along with Langford, and had been handed over on Blandina's marriage, in excellent condition, to Nanspian, and had gone back ever since he had enjoyed it. This angered Langford, though he knew Chimsworthy would never be his. 'This is the sort of tricks to which young Larry is reared, which he will play with Langford. As the bull gambols, so capers the calf.'

Hillary did not relish the visits of Taverner to the Look-out Stone. He thought, and thought rightly, that Langford was criticising unfavourably his management of the estate. He was conscious that the farm had deteriorated, but he laid the blame on the weather and the badness of construction of the drains, on everything but himself. 'How can you expect drains to last, put down as they are, one flat stone on edge and another leaning on it aslant? Down it goes with the weight of earth atop, and the passage is choked. I'll eat a Jew without mint-sauce if a drain so constructed will last twenty years.' Chimsworthy could never go to Taverner, what right then had he to grumble if it were in bad order?

When Langford came to the Look-out Stone Hillary soon heard of it, and went to him in his shirt-sleeves, pipe in mouth, and with a jug of cyder in his hand. Then some such a greeting as this ensued:

'Trespassing again, Taverner?'

'Looking at the land over which I've walked, and where I've weeded many a day, with my father, before you was thought of in Bratton Clovelly.'

Then Hillary drew the pipe from his lips, and, raking the horizon with the sealing-waxed end, said, 'Fine land, yonder.'

'Moor—naught but moor,' answered Langford disparagingly.

'No cawding of sheep on peaty moor,' said Nanspian triumphantly.

'No fattening of bullocks on heather,' replied Taverner. 'It is wet in Devon, it is wetter in Cornwall.'

'Wetter! That is not possible. Here we live on the rose of a watering-can, pillowed among bogs.'

'There are worse things than water,' sneered Langford, pointing to the jug.

'Ah!' said Hillary in defence. 'Sour is the land that grows sour apples and sour folks.'

'Heaven made the apples—they are good enough. Man makes the cyder —which is evil. Thus it is with other good gifts, we pervert them to our bad ends.'

This was the formula gone through, with slight variations, whenever the brothers-in-law met at the granite seat. A little ruffle of each other, but it went no further.

Hillary Nanspian was a talker, not loud but continuous. He had a rich, low, murmuring voice, with which he spoke out of one side of his mouth, whilst he inhaled tobacco through the other. It was pleasant to listen to, like the thrum of a bumble-bee or the whirr of a winnowing fan. The eyes closed, the head nodded, and sleep ensued. But every now and then Hillary uttered an oath, for he was not a man to wear a padlock on his lips, and then the dozing listener woke with a start. When that listener was Taverner, he uttered his protest. 'The word is uncalled for, Hillary; change it for one that sounds like it, and is inoffensive and unmeaning.'

There was much difference in the way in which the two men behaved when angered. Hillary was hot and blazed up in a sudden outburst. He was easily angered, but soon pacified, unless his pride were hurt. Taverner, on the other hand, though equally to take umbrage, took it in another fashion. He turned sallow, said little, and brooded over his wrong. If an opportunity offered to resent it, it was not allowed to pass, however long after the event. One evening the brothers-in-law were at the Look-out Stone. Hillary was standing with his foot on the block on which Taverner sat.

'I'll tell you what,' said Nanspian, 'I wish I'd got a few thousands to spare. Swaddledown is for sale, and the farm joins mine, and would be handy for stock.'

'And I wish I could buy Bannadon. That will be in the market shortly, but I cannot unless you repay me what you have borrowed.'

'Can't do that just now; not comfortably, you understand.'

'Then what is the good of your scheming to buy Swaddledown? A man without teeth mustn't pick nuts.'

'And what is the good of your wanting Bannadon when you have as much as you can manage at Langford? A man with his mouth full mustn't take a second bite till he's swallowed the first.'

Then neither spoke for a few moments. Presently, however, Hillary drew a long whiff, and blew the smoke before him. Slowly he pulled the pipe from between his lips, and with the end of the stem pointed down the valley. 'It would be something to be able to call those fields my own.'

'That would be pulling on boots to hide the stocking full of holes,' sneered Taverner. Hillary coloured, and his eyes twinkled. 'There is no picking feathers off a toad, or clothes off a naked man,' he muttered; 'and if you squeeze a crab-apple you get only sourness. If I were not your brother-in-law I shouldn't put up with your words. But you can't help it. Sloes and blackberries grow in the same hedge, and their natures are as they began. Older they grow, they grow either sweeter or sourer.'

'Ah!' retorted Taverner, 'out of the acre some grow wheat and others nettles.'

'It is all very well your talking,' said Hillary, putting his thumbs in his waistcoat arm-holes, and expanding. 'You, no doubt, have made money, one way or other. I have not; but then, I am not a screw. I am a free-handed, open man. God forbid that I should be a screw!'

'A screw holds together and a wedge drives apart,' said Taverner.

'I don't know,' said Hillary, looking across lovingly at the Swaddledown fields, 'but I may be able to find the money. My credit is not so low that I need look far. If you will not help me others will.'

'How can you raise it? on a mortgage? You cannot without young Hillary's consent, and he is not of age.'

'Luck will come my way some time,' said Nanspian. 'Luck is not nailed to one point of the compass, brother Langford. Don't you flatter yourself that it always goes to you. Luck veers as the wind.'

'That is true, but as the wind here sets three days out of four from the west, so does luck set most time towards the thrifty man.'

'Sooner or later it will turn to me.'

'I know what you mean. I've heard tell of what you have said to the farmers when warmed with liquor. The wind don't blow over a thistlehead without carrying away some of its down and dropping it where least wanted. I've heard your boasts, they are idle—idle as thistledown. Do you think you'll ever succeed to Langford? I'll live to see your burying.'

'My burying won't help you to Chimsworthy,' retorted Hillary. 'My Larry stands in your way. Heigh! I said it! The luck is coming my way already!' he exclaimed eagerly. He put down his foot, placed both palms on the slab of granite, and leaned over it.

'Not a moment before it is needed,' said Taverner. 'You've had some bad falls, and they'd have been breakdown tumbles but for my help. I suppose you must let Swaddledown go; it's a pity too, lying handy as the button at the flap of your pocket.'

'She is coming my way as fast as she can!'

15

'What, Swaddledown?'

'No! Luck! Look! running right into my hands. The money-spinner!'

'The money-spinner!' Taverner started to his feet. 'Where? Whither is she running?'

'Stand out of the sunlight, will you!' exclaimed Hillary. 'How can I see and secure her with your shadow cast across the stone?'

'Where is she?'

'I tell you she is making direct for me. I knew the luck would come if I waited. Curse you! Get on one side, will you?'

'Don't swear,' said Langford, standing at the other end of the granite slab, and resting his hands on it. 'The money-spinner is a tickle (touchy) beast, and may take offence at a godless word. I see her, she has turned. You've scared her with your oaths, and now she is running towards me.'

'She's going to fetch some of your luck and bring it to my pocket; she's on the turn again.'

'No, she is not. She is making for me, not you.'

'But she is on my stone. She has brought the luck to me.'

'She may be on your stone now, but she is leaving it for my hand, as fast as her red legs can carry her.'

'You're luring her away from me, are you?' cried Hillary, blazing as red as any money-spinner.

'Luring! She's running her natural course as sure as a fox runs before the wind.'

'Stand out of the sun! It is the ugly shade you cast that chills her. She goes where she may be warmest.'

'Out of thine own mouth thou speakest thy condemnation,' scoffed Langford. 'Of course she goes to the warmest corner, and which is warmest, my pocket or thine?—the full or the empty?'

'The spinner is on my stone, and I will have her!'cried Hillary.

'Your stone!—yes, yours because you got it and Chimsworthy away from me.'

'The spinner is by your hand!' roared Nanspian, and with an oath he threw himself across the stone and swept the surface with his hands.

Langford uttered an exclamation of anger. 'You have crushed—you have killed her! There is an end of luck to you, you long-tailed Cornish ourang-outang!'

Hillary Nanspian staggered back. His face became dark with rage. He opened his lips, but was inarticulate for a moment; then he roared, 'You say that, do you, you ——, that let yourself be led and tongue-lashed by your housekeeper.'

'Our friendship is at an end,' said Langford, turning livid, and his dark bushy brows met across his forehead. 'Never shall you set foot in Langford now.'

'Never! It will come to my Larry, and I'll drink your burying ale there yet.'

'Larry shall never have it.'

'You can't keep him out,' exclaimed Hillary.

'Do not be so sure of that,' saidTaverner.

'I am sure. I have seen the parchments.'

'I know them better than you,' laughed Langford. Then he went to the stile to leave the field.

'I'll have the law of you,' shouted Hillary; 'you are trespassing on my land.'

'I trespassing!' mocked Langford; 'this is a stile leading to

Swaddledown.'

'There is no right of way here. This is a private stile leading only to the Look-out Stone. I will have the law of you, I swear.'

Thus it was that the friendship of twenty-two years was broken, and the brothers-in-law became declared and deadly enemies. The friendship was broken irremediably by an insect almost microscopic—a little scarlet spider no larger than a mustard-seed, invested by popular superstition with the power of spinning money in the pocket of him who secures it.

CHAPTER III

WELLON'S CAIRN.

Whilst Hillary Nanspian and Taverner Langford were falling out over a minute red spider, Hillary junior, or Larry as he was called by his intimates, was talking to Honor Luxmore in a nook of the rubble of Wellon's Cairn.

Wellon's Cairn is a great barrow, or tumulus on Broadbury, not far from Langworthy. Its original name has been lost. Since a certain Wellon was hung in chains on a gallows set up on this mound for the murder of three women it has borne his name.

The barrow was piled up of stones and black peat earth, and was covered with gorse, so that the old British warrior who lay beneath may indeed be said to have made his bed in glory. The gorse brake not only blazed as fire, but streamed forth perfume like a censer. Only on the summit was a bare space, where the gallows had stood, and Wellon had dropped piecemeal, and been trodden by the sheep into the black soil.

On the south-west side, facing the sun, was a hollow. Treasure-seekers had dug into the mound. Tradition said that therein lay a hero in harness of gold. The panoply that wrapped him round was indeed of gold, but it was the gold of the ever-blooming gorse. Having found nothing but a few flint flakes and broken sherds, the seekers had abandoned the cairn, without filling up the cavity. This had fallen in, and was lined with moss and short grass, and fringed about with blushing heath and blazing gorse.

In this bright and fragrant hollow, from the world, and sheltered from the wind that wafted down on her the honey breath of the furze, and exposed to the warmth of the declining sun, sat Honor Luxmore; and near her, not seated, but leaning against the side of the excavation, stood Hillary junior talking to her.

Hillary was like his father, well built, fair-haired, and flushed with life. His eyes were blue, quick and honest, sparkling with fun; and his bearing was that of the heir of Chimsworthy and Langford. There was unmistakable self-reliance in his face, making up, in measure, for lack of superior intelligence.

Honor Luxmore demands a fuller account than young Hillary.

Some way down the lane from Wellon's Cairn stood a cottage. This cottage was constructed on the bank or hedge above the roadway, so that the door was reached by a flight of steps, partly cut in the rock, partly constructed of stone. A handrail assisted ascent and descent. The cottage seemed to have taken refuge up the side of the bank to escape from the water in the lane. Actually the roadway was cut through shale to some depth, leaving the cottage on the true surface of the land. The road had no doubt in part been artificially cut, but certainly it had been also scooped in part by the water, which, issuing from the joints of the shale, converted it into a watercourse. The sides of the road were rich with moss and fern, and the moss and fern were spangled with drops that oozed out of the rock. Below the steps was a spring, in a hole scooped in the side of the loose, shaley rock.

The cottage itself was of cob, whitewashed, with a thatched roof, brown and soft as the fur of a mole. The windows were small and low, In this cottage lived Oliver Luxmore, a man poor in everything but children, and of these he possessed more than he knew how to provide for. The cottage was like a hive. Flaxen-haired boys and girls of all ages might be seen pouring out on their way to school, or swarming home in the evening. They were all pretty children, with dazzling blue eyes and clear complexions and fair hair, from the youngest, a little maid of three, upwards; and what was better than beauty, they were patterns of neatness and cleanliness. According to the proverb, cleanliness comes next to goodliness, but these little Luxmores were both cleanly and goodly. The goodliness they drew from their parents, but the cleanliness was due to Honor, the eldest daughter of Oliver Luxmore, who stood to her brothers and sisters in the place of mother, for the wife of Luxmore had died three years ago, just after the birth of her youngest.

The father was a carrier, who drove a van on Fridays to Tavistock, and on Saturdays to Okehampton, the market-days at these respective places. On the other week-days he worked for the farmers, doing odd jobs, and so earning money for the sustenance of his many children.

Oliver Luxmore was a quiet, dreamy, unenergetic man, who was hampered by a belief that he was the right heir to a good property, which would certainly be his if only he were able to find the necessary registers, but what these registers were, whether of marriage or birth, he was uncertain. At the extreme limits of the parish, in a pretty situation, lay a good house of Queen Anne's reign, with some fine trees, and traces of gardens, and a fishpond, called Coombe Park, which had belonged to the Luxmoores or Luxmores. But this property had been sold, and Oliver maintained that if he had had but one hundred pounds wherewith to find the registers, Coombe Park could not have been sold, and he would be a squire there, with a good fortune. He had visited a lawyer in Okehampton, and another at Tavistock, to ask them to take up his on speculation, but Oliver's ideas were so hazy as to his pedigree, never resolving themselves into definite statements of fact, that both one and the other declined to touch his claim unless they were given some certain ground on which to work.

Then he went to the Rector of Bratton, and with his help extracted all the entries of births, marriages, and deaths of the Luxmores—pages of them, showing that from the beginning of the sixteenth century the name had abounded there, and belonged to or was assumed by persons of all ranks and conditions. Then Oliver took this list to the Okehampton lawyer.

'Look here,' said he, 'my eldest daughter is called Honor, and in 1662 John Luxmore, gentleman, and Temperance, his wife, had a daughter baptised called Honor. That's proof, is it not?'

'Why was your daughter christened by this name?'

'Well, you see my wife was Honor, and so we called our first girl after her.'

This may be taken as a specimen that will suffice of Oliver's evidences, and as a justification of the solicitors declining to take up his claim.

'It is one hundred pounds that is wanted to do it,' said Oliver Luxmore. 'If I had that to spend on the registers, it would come right enough. I always heard my father say that if we had our rights we shouldn't be in the cottage in Water Lane.'

Oliver spent money and wasted time over his ineffectual attempts to prove his descent and establish his rights, but he had not the slightest idea what to search for and how to search. He did not even know his grandfather's Christian-name, but believed it began with a J, for he had an old linen shirt that was marked in the tail with J. L., and was so strong and sound that he wore it still. J. might stand for John, or James, or Joseph, or Jeremiah. But then he was not *quite* sure the shirt had belonged to his grandfather, but he had heard his mother say she believed it had.

On days when he might have been earning money he would wander away to Coombe Park, prowl round the estate estimating its value, or go into the house to drink cyder with the yeoman who now owned and occupied it, to tell him that his claim might yet be established, and to assure him that he would deal honourably and liberally with him when he turned him out. The yeoman and his wife regarded him as something of a nuisance, but nevertheless treated him with respect. There was no knowing, they said, but that he might prove in the end to be the heir, and then where would they be? Oliver would have liked to see the title-deeds, but of these he was not allowed a glimpse, though he could not have read them had he seen them, or made his claim the clearer if he had been able to read them.

We have said that Oliver Luxmore worked for the farmers on the days of the week on which he was not carrying between Bratton and Tavistock and Okehampton; but Thursdays and Mondays were broken days. On Thursdays he went about soliciting orders, and on Mondays he went about distributing parcels. Thus he had only two clear days for jobbing. The work of a carrier is desultory, and unfits him for manual labour and for persevering work. He gets into idle, gossiping ways. When he picks up a parcel or a passenger he has to spend a quarter of an hour discussing what has to be done with the parcel, and has to settle the passenger comfortably among the parcels, without the passenger impinging on the parcels, or the parcels incommoding the passenger.

Oliver was an obliging, amiable man. In the front of his van was a seat, the top of which could be raised on hinges, and in which he deposited watches that went to be cleaned, books of the Reading Club that travelled between subscribers, medicine bottles and boxes of pills, ribbons, brooches, and other delicate goods. The lid of this box was sat on and kept secure by Oliver. He was devoid of humour. To every commission, to every joke, to every reprimand, he had but one answer, 'Certainly, certainly, very true.'

'Oliver,' said Nanspian one day, 'I can suggest to you a means of increasing your income. Put a sitting of eggs under you when you go to market, and sell the young chickens when you get there.'

'Certainly, certainly, sir, very true,' was his civil reply, without a muscle of his face moving.

'Oh, Mr. Luxmore!' exclaimed Mrs. Robbins, the rectoress, 'this is the same book you brought me last month from the parsonage at Maristowe. I have had it and returned it, and now you bring it me again. Mind it goes back on Friday; and you shall not be paid for your trouble, as I cannot be expected to read the same book over twice.'

'Certainly, certainly, ma'am, very true.'

'Oh, Mr. Luxmore,' said Mrs. Veale, 'you are to mind and match me the silk, cut on the cross, and if the shade be out, I won't take it, you must return it, and pay for it from your own pocket.'

'Certainly, certainly, ma'am.'

'The Vivid,' as Mr. Luxmore's van was called, belied its name. There was no vividity (pass the word) about it. It went slowly up hill, because the horse had so much to draw. It went slower down hill, because it had to back against such a prodigious weight, descending by natural velocity. There was not a mile—not half a mile—of level road between Bratton Clovelly and the market-towns.

The carrier's horse was a rough creature, brown, with a long tail, thick mane, and coarse hair about the fetlocks, of the colour of tow. It lived in a precarious manner; the children cut grass in the hedges for it, and it was sometimes turned out on Broadbury, with hobbles on its feet. It ate the refuse of Luxmore's vegetable garden, the turnip-tops, the potato parings, the maggot-nibbled outer cabbage leaves, and the decayed apples from his trees. Once, when the horse had knocked his nose, and Luxmore had put a linseed poultice over it, in a bit of sacking tied round the head with four stout tapes, when his back was turned the horse curled his tongue out of his mouth, detached the poultice, and ate it, linseed, sacking, and tapes, to the last grain and thread. There was nothing but stones that horse would not eat. He bit away great pieces from his manger. He took a bite out of Luxmore's trousers, he gnawed the bark off the cherry-tree by his gate, he gobbled up nettles, thistles, furze, as though his appetite were as vitiated as an East Indian's.

Oliver Luxmore had to put up with a good many bad debts: his business did not bring him in much money; he was never able to lay by a penny: how could he with so many mouths to feed at home? Honor would have been unable to make both ends meet unless she had been a manager. The family would have been better off if Charles, the eldest son, two years the senior of Honor, had fulfilled his duty to his own. But Charles, having reached the full wage-earning age, had enlisted, and was away on foreign service. His father and sister did not even know where he was, for he had not troubled himself to write since his departure. Charles had always been a wild and headstrong boy who needed a firm hand over him to direct him right. But Oliver Luxmore's hand was weak, and the mother, a shrewd, painstaking woman of decided character, had made the boy obstinate and sulky, by exerting over him the authority which should have been exercised by his father.

After the death of his wife, Oliver remained as weak as during her life, very good-natured, and so pliant as to bend to the wills of his children, even to that of his youngest, Temperance, aged three. The family would indisputably have run wild, and his affairs gone to ruin, had not Honor assumed her mother's place, and ruled the little house with energy and decision. Her rule was firm but loving, and few of the children ventured to disobey her, not even the thirteen-year-old Joseph, or her next sister, Kate, aged seventeen; no, not even her father, Oliver; indeed he was the least difficult to manage of all. There were nine children in all. Charles, Honor, Kate, Joseph, have already been mentioned, so has little Temperance the baby. Between Joseph and Temperance came Pattie, that is Patience, Willy, Martha, and Charity. The children were all pretty and well-conducted. Charles was no longer a child. He was away. He therefore is not reckoned among those who were pretty and well-conducted.

Honor was tall; her bearing very erect; her well-knit, vigorous frame, the glance of her clear hazel eyes, her firm mouth, all combined to inspire respect and insure submission. The respectability of her father, the honesty of her brothers and sisters were due to Honor, and to Honor alone. But for her presence in the house everything would have gone wrong. Kate was too lively and careless to manage it, the others too young, her father helpless. Had she not been there to keep home orderly, and the children neat, Oliver would have drifted to the tavern to bury his troubles in the ale-can, and the little ones would have sunk into squalor and strife, and struggled out of childhood into misery, beggary, and vice.

The children had inherited from their father blue eyes and very fair hair; they had lovely complexions, and clear, bright colour; some of them had certainly derived from him also an inertness of character which left them and their futures at the mercy of the persons and the chances that should surround or fall in their way. This was not the case with Kate, who had character of her own, though very diverse from that of her eldest sister. Kate promised to be the beauty of the family. Her blue eyes twinkled with mirth and mischief, like summer seas. She had a roguish dimple in her cheeks, and an expression of consciousness of her good looks on her face.

Honor was different in appearance, as in character, from the rest. She hardly seemed to belong to the family. She had hair the colour of barley-sugar, and hazel-brown eyes. She looked every one whom she addressed straight in the face, and was absolutely void of vanity; she asked no admiration like Kate. She was contemptuously indifferent to her looks, and yet she was never untidy. All the rest were better dressed than herself. She never gave herself new clothes; she had an old store of her mother's to draw from for her own clothing; but though her gown was antiquated and often patched, it was never ragged, never had tape and thread ends hanging from it. She had inherited her grandmother's scarlet cloak, and was the last person in that neighbourhood to wear such a garment. This she only wore on Sundays, but she wore it on every Sunday, summer as well as winter, when she went to church. She also wore red stockings, and as she was taller than her mother, and her mother's gowns could not be lengthened, a good deal of red stocking showed. She wore these stockings simply because they were her mother's and had to be worn out, and because Kate objected to them for her own feet. Perhaps it was the shortness of the skirts that gave to Honor a look of length of red limb below the scarlet cloak a little grotesque, that occasioned the boys of Bratton to nickname her 'the Red Spider.'

The mischievous Kate teased her by asserting that she got her name from her hair; but Honor's hair was not red, it was not even chestnut brown, it was golden brown, like beech-leaves in autumn—a very rare, but a beautiful colour. It was all one to Honor what hair she had, all one to her what the boys styled her. No girl could be jealous of her; she had no eyes for the lads, her whole heart, her every thought was centred in home. As the chapter-house of a cathedral is built in a circle and leans on one central pillar, and as the fall of that pillar would insure the ruin of the house, so was it with the cottage of the Luxmores—on her it rested. This she knew, and the little self-consciousness she possessed was the consciousness that on her all leaned for support, and to her owed their uprightness.

'What a lot of socks and stockings you have got on the furze bushes about you,' said Hillary.

'Yes—like to have. There are so many little feet at home that tread holes.'

'You must be glad that they are two-footed, not four-footed animals, those brothers and sisters of yours.'

'I am, or I could not darn their stockings, much less knit them.'

Hillary thought a moment; then he said, looking at a pair of very much darned red stockings hung over a branch of heather, 'You know they call you the Red Spider, and they say true. The Red Spider brings luck wherever she goes. I am sure you are the money-spinner in your house.'

'I!' exclaimed the girl, who coloured slightly, and looked up; 'I—I spin, but never money.'

'Well, you bring luck.'

'I keep out ill-luck,' she answered with confidence; 'I can do no more, but that is something, and that takes me all my time. I have hardly leisure to sleep.'

'Why have you brought all these stockings out on the Down? Are you going to convert Wellon's Cairn into a second-hand mercer's shop?'

'Larry, in spite of proverb to the contrary, I am forced to do two things at a time. I have Diamond to watch as well as stockings to darn. The poor beast is not well, and I have brought him from the stable. The little ones are at school, except of course Temperance, and Kate is with her cutting grass in the lane for Diamond.'

'What would you do if you lost Diamond?' asked young Hillary.

'O Larry, don't even suggest such an evil. If you whistle you call up wind, and if you whisper the name of the devil he looks in at the door. We got into debt buying Diamond, and it took us three years to work our way out. Now we are clear, and it would be too dreadful to get into debt again. You know, Larry, what the mothers do with children who have the thrush. They pass them under a bramble that grows with a loop into the ground. Like enough the little creatures lose the thrush, but they carry away scratches. Debt, to my thinking, is like treatment; you get rid of one evil by sticking yourself full of thorns. So take my advice, and never get into debt.'

'I'm not like to,' laughed the young man, 'with Chimsworthy behind me and Langford before me.'

'Never reckon on what you've not got,' said Honor. 'That's like buying the hogshead before the apples have set, or killing a pig without having the pickle-tub. Langford is not yours, any more than Coombe Park is ours.'

'Langford must come to us Nanspians some day, you know, Honor. Not that I reckon on it. God forbid. May Uncle Taverner live for ever. But it gives a chap confidence to know that a large estate will come to him in the end.'

'Don't reckon on that,' said Honor.

'It can't fail. It stands so in the deeds.'

'But Mr. Langford might marry.'

Hillary would have burst into a hearty laugh at the idea, had not Honor laid her hand on his arm to arrest him, and raised the forefinger of the other to impose silence.

Sitting up on its hind legs, in a begging posture, at the mouth of the excavation, was a *white hare*. It looked at the young people for a moment, doubtingly, inquiringly. Then Hillary stirred, and with a flash it was gone.

Hillary exclaimed, 'O Honor! is it not the picture of Mrs. Veale?'

CHAPTER IV.

THE WHITE HARE.

'I have seen the white hare before, several times,' said Honor Luxmore.

'You have? Do you know what folks say?'

'They say that it is unlucky to see a white hare; but I think nothing of that.'

'I do not mean that,' said Hillary, laughing. 'But they say that when a witch goes on her errands she takes this shape. Perhaps, Honor,' he went on with roguery in his twinkling eyes, 'Mrs. Veale is off over the Down in quest of her master. He has gone to the Look-out Stone to have a talk to my father.'

'Nonsense, Larry. I put no credit in those tales of witches; besides, I never heard that Mrs. Veale was one—not properly.'

'She is white with pink eyes, and so is the hare,' argued Hillary, 'and spiteful she is, certainly. I hope, if that were her, she won't be bringing mischief to you or to me. We shall see. If that were her, Uncle Taverner will be coming home directly. Folks say that he is afraid of her tongue, and that is the only thing in heaven or hell he is afraid of.'

Honor uttered an exclamation of surprise and alarm. A black ungainly figure stood before them, black against the glowing western sky. She recovered herself at once and rose respectfully. Hillary turned and recognised his uncle.

'Well, Uncle Taverner!' he exclaimed, 'you have come on us suddenly. We were just talking about you.'

'Ah' answered Langford, leaning on his stick and lowering at him, 'leave me out of your talk and your calculations altogether. I dare say you have been reckoning on my shoes, and how well they would fit your young feet. No, no! no feet of yours shall ever be thrust into them.' Then seeing that Hillary was disconcerted, he laughed a harsh, bitter laugh. 'Your father and I have parted for ever. We have quarrelled; I will not speak to him more. To you I speak now for the last time also. As Nanspian has split with Langford, Chimsworthy and Langford will not splice. Remember that. Go to work, young man, go to work, instead of standing idling here. Your father is in my debt, and you must help him to earn the money to pay me off.' Then he turned to Honor, and said, 'Why are you here, instead of watching your horse? Diamond is down in the gravel-pit, on his side, dead or dying.'

Honor sprang up with a cry.

'The white hare,' said Hillary, 'has brought the ill-luck—to both of us at once.'

Neither of the young people gave another thought to Taverner Langford. Honor was in distress about the horse, and Hillary was desirous of assisting her. He accompanied her to the spot, a hole dug in the surface of the moor for rubble wherewith to mend the road. Diamond had either made his way into it by the cart road, or had fallen over the edge. He lay on his side panting.

'Poor fellow,' said Hillary gravely, 'Diamond is done for.'

'Oh, I ought not to have let him from my sight,' cried Honor, stung with self-reproach.

'You could do nothing for him,' said the young man. 'He is not dying from your neglect. Look here, Honor, do you see that hoof-print? He walked in, he did not fall over the edge. Every beast when it feels death approach tries to hide itself, as though it were ashamed—as though death were a crime. It is so, Honor.'

'O Larry! What can I do? What can I do for poor Diamond?'

'You can do nothing but pat him and let him go out of the world with a word of love.'

'I will do that. I will indeed!' Then she caressed the old horse, and stroked its cheek and nose, and spoke to it tenderly. Diamond raised his head, snuffed, rubbed his head against his young mistress, then laid it down again on the stones and died.

Honor's tears flowed, but she was not one to make a demonstration of distress. She said: 'I must go home, Larry, and get supper ready for the children. I can do nothing here now.'

'I am very sorry for you,' said Hillary, showing more emotion than she; 'I am indeed, Honor. I know what a terrible loss this will be to your father, and he is too proud a man to go round with a brief. Put your hand to mine, Honor; we shall always be good friends, and I will do what I can for you; but it cannot be much now that Uncle Taverner is across with us, and about to exact his money. I will tell you what. I will get my father to lend you our horse Derby for awhile, till we can scheme what is to be done. I wish I'd got a quarter of an acre of land of my own, and I would sell it and give you the money wherewith to buy another horse. I would, in truth and sincerity, Honor.'

'I am sure of that,' answered the girl; 'I know I can always trust to your good-will and kind offices. Good-bye! I must go.'

Then Hillary went slowly homewards. The sun had gone down in the west, and the sky was full of after glory. A few level bars, steps of vivid fire, were drawn against the sky, and there was, as it were, a pavement of sapphire strewn with the down from a flamingo. The moor stood with every furze-bush on its margin and two small cairns on the edge blotted black against the blaze. As Hillary descended from the moor he got into the Chimsworthy Lane, shadowed by a plantation of Scottish pines his father had made twenty years ago, and which stood up high enough to intercept the light.

'Poor Honor!' mused Hillary. 'Whatever will she and her father and all

31

those little uns do without the horse? A carrier without a horse is a helpless animal. I don't like to ask my father too much for the Luxmores, and seem hot about them, or he will be thinking I am in love with Honor, which I am not. Some chaps think a young fellow cannot speak to a girl, or even look at her, without being in love with her. I like Honor well enough, as a friend, but no more.'

The road was very rough, he could not descend fast because of the loose stones. In rainy weather the way was a watercourse, and the water broke up the shale rock that formed the floor and scattered it in angular fragments over the road.

'What a ridiculous notion, that I should be in love with a carrier's daughter! I a Nanspian of Chimsworthy, and heir——' he stopped. 'No—that part is not to be, though how Uncle Taverner will do us out of Langford is more than I can imagine. That he should marry and have a family is clean too ridiculous! Confound that stone! It nigh turned and broke my ankle. If Honor's father had Coombe Park it would be another matter. Then, possibly, I might think of her in a different way; but—a cottage girl!—a carrier's daughter! Luxmore is not a bad name. But then they have the name and nothing else. I'll cut myself a stick, or I shall be down on my nose. I should not care for Honor to see me to-morrow with a broken nose. These pines may be a shelter, but they cast a very black shadow, and the rabbits breed in the plantation like midges in a duck-pond.'

He cut himself a stick and went on. 'If Honor were here, I should be forced to lend her a hand, and then if father or any one were to meet us, there'd be laughter and jokes. I'm mighty glad Honor is not here.'

Presently he got beyond the pines.

The hedges were high, the way still dark.

'Good heavens!' he exclaimed, 'the white hare again!'

As he cried out, a white animal ran up the lane, passed him and disappeared.

'Confound it,' said Hillary. 'I wish I had not seen that. Why——what have we here?'

He ran forward. In the lane, across it, where the stile to the Look-out Stone allowed a streak of western light to stream across the road, lay Hillary Nanspian senior, insensible, on his face, with the broken cyder jug in his hand.

'Father! what ails you? Speak!' cried Hillary junior. He tried to lift the old man; he could raise but not carry him. The anger aroused by his contention with Langford had brought on a fit.

CHAPTER V.

'TIMEO DANAOS ET DONA FERENTES.'

Honor Luxmore sat near the window, weaving a hamper out of willow twigs. Her sister Kate was similarly engaged. By the fire sat Oliver, smoking and watching the smouldering peat on the hearth. The sisters earned money by making baskets. Down in the bottoms, in the marshy land, grew willow-bushes; and they were allowed by the farmers to cut as much as they needed free of charge. Towards Christmas, indeed from the 1st of October, there was a demand for 'maunds,' in which to send away as presents. Honor, Kate, and even some of the younger children could plait withies into hampers, which their father took into Launceston and Tavistock on market-days and sold. Little figures make up long sums, and so the small proceeds of the basket-weaving formed no inconsiderable profit in the year, out of which Honor was able to clothe her sister Kate and one of the other children.

Silence had lasted some time in the room; Oliver leaned forward with his elbows on his knees, dreamily watching the fire. At last he said, 'Whatever I am to do for a horse I cannot tell. I've sold the carcase to Squire Impey to feed the hounds with for a half-sovereign, and the skin for another ten shillings. That is all I got for Diamond. I suppose I shall have to give up carrying and go on the land. To think of that, I that should be in Coombe Park riding about in a gilded coach with four cream horses and long tails and a powdered coachman on the box—that I should become a day labourer for lack of a horse!'

'Never mind about Coombe Park, father. It is of no use looking down a well for a lost shilling. Young Mr. Larry Nanspian will lend you a horse for a while.'

'What will that avail?' asked Oliver disconsolately. 'It is like sucking eggs when you've got the consumption. It puts off the dying a few days, but it don't cure.'

'The last horse was paid for. You are not in debt.'

'Ah! but then I had not so many little ones growing up. I could be trusted to pay. But now they consume every penny I earn.'

'They cost more as they grow up, but they also earn something. I've a mind to do this, father. You know I've been asked by several gentlefolk to go to their houses and reseat their cane-bottomed chairs, but I've never liked to go because of the distance, and because I wouldn't leave the house and the children. But now Kate is old enough to take my place and do such little matters as are needed here during the day, I will go about and do the chairs.

Oliver Luxmore laughed. 'You'll never buy a horse with cane bottoms. No, that won't do. I'll give up carrying and go work on the roads. You don't know what grand new macadamised roads are being laid out; they are carrying them round slopes, where before they went straight up. They are filling in bottoms, and slicing into hills. Thousands upon thousands of pounds are being spent, and there are whole gangs of men engaged upon them.'

'No, father, you are too old for that work. Besides, those who go to the road-making are the rough and riotous young fellows who want high wages, and who spend their money in drink. No, such society is not for you.'

'I don't see that,' said the father. 'As you say, the wages are very high; I am not so old that I cannot work.'

'You are unaccustomed to the kind of work.'

'I should get into the way of it, and I am no drunkard to waste my money.'

'But you are a Luxmore.'

Oliver held up his head. That last was an unanswerable argument. He considered for a while, and then he said, 'I cannot borrow the money of Mr. Nanspian, he is ill. It is, of course, useless my asking Mr. Langford, he is not a lending, but a taking man.'

'If we worked out the first debt, we can work out the second,' said Honor. 'I know that you can get nothing from Chimsworthy, and I do not suppose you can get anything from Langford, nevertheless you might try. Mr. Langford knows you to be an industrious and a conscientious man. He has but to look in your face, father, to be sure that you would rather be cheated than cheat any one. Try Mr. Taverner Langford to-morrow.'

'It is no good,' sighed Oliver. 'Only wear out shoe leather for nothing. You go if you think anything of the chance. Folks say, walk with Hope, or you are walking backwards.'

'I—I go to Mr. Langford!'

'No need for that, when I have come to you,' answered a voice at the open window.

Honor started, looked up, and saw Taverner Langford there, looking at her, and then at Oliver.

'Won't you step in and take a chair, sir?' asked Honor, rising and moving towards the door.

'No, I am well where I am,' answered Taverner, leaning his elbows on the bottom of the window and peering in. He wore a broad-brimmed hat, that shadowed the upper part of his face, but out of this shadow shone his eyes with phosphoric light.

'Father!' exclaimed Honor, 'here is Mr. Langford.'

Oliver had risen and stood with his pipe in one hand leaning against one jamb of the chimney, looking wonderingly at the visitor. Langford had ascended the steps from the lane, and thus had appeared suddenly before the Luxmores.

From the window no one that passed was visible unless he were seated on the top of a load of hay carted along the lane from the harvest-field.

Oliver Luxmore went to the window, and, like his daughter, asked, 'Will you step inside, sir?'

'No, thank you,' answered Langford, 'I can talk very comfortably standing where I am. I know you to be a sensible man, Luxmore, and to have your eyes about you, and your ears open. There is no man goes about the country so much as you. They say that in a town the barber knows all the news, and in the country the carrier. Now I'll tell you what I want, Luxmore, and perhaps you'll do me the favour to help me to what I want. I'm short of hands, and I want a trusty fellow who can act as cattle-driver for me. I won't have a boy. Boys over-drive and hurt the cattle. I must have a man. Do you know of one who will suit?'

Oliver shook his head. 'I don't know that I do, and I don't know that I don't.'

'You are talking riddles, Luxmore. What do you mean?'

'Well, sir,' answered the carrier with a sigh, 'my meaning is this. Poor Diamond is dead, and I am thinking of giving up the carrying trade.'

'Giving up the "Vivid"! You are not in your senses, man.'

'Ah, sir, how am I to buy a new horse? The price is up and money is scarce—leastways with me. Horses ain't to be bought on promises no more

36

than they are to be reared on wind.'

'Want a horse, do you? Of course the "Vivid" won't go by herself except down hill, and that is what every one and every thing can do unassisted. It is the getting up hill that costs a strain. Ah, Luxmore, I could show you two men, one going up and the other down, going down as fast as the laden van on Rexhill, without a horse to back against it. You've only to look to Chimsworthy to see that. I need not say in which direction to turn your eyes to see the contrary.'

He pushed up his hat and looked at the carrier, then at Honor. He did not deign to cast a passing glance at Kate.

'Then, sir,' said Oliver, 'if the worst came to the worst—I mean, sir, begging your pardon, and no offence intended, if I could not get another horse, and where it is to come from the Lord Almighty only knows—I'd have to work for my living some other way, and I might be glad to take service with you. I was even thinking on going to the roads that be making, but Honor won't hear of that, so I reckon it can't be.'

'No,' answered Taverner, with his eyes resting on Honor, 'no, she is quite right. Your proper place is at home with the family. The men on the roads are a wild lot.'

'So she said,' the carrier put in humbly, 'and of course Honor knows.'

'Now look you here, Luxmore,' said Taverner, 'I'm not a man to squander and give away, as every one in Bratton knows, but I'm not as hard as they are pleased to say, and where a worthy man is in need, and no great risk is seen by myself, and I'm not out of pocket, I don't mind helping him. I do not say but what I'll let you have my grey for keep. She's not an infant. There's not much gambol about her, but there is a deal of work. You shall have her for awhile; and pay me ten shillings a week, as hire. That is a favourable offer, is it not?'

The carrier stood silent with astonishment. Honor's cheeks flushed with pleasure and surprise, so did those of Kate.

37

'Your grey!' exclaimed Luxmore. 'I know her well. She's worth five-and-twenty pounds.'

'She may be. I do not know. I will not consider that. I do not want her just now, and shall be glad to lend her for her keep and a trifle. You are an honest man. Your family is like mine—come down in the world.'

'Ah!' exclaimed the carrier, raising his head proudly, 'I reckon Coombe Park is where I should be, and all I want wherewith to get it is a hundred pounds and a register.'

'That may be,' said Taverner; 'there were Luxmores in Bratton as long as there have been Langfords, and that goes back hundreds of years. I do not want to see you fall to the ground. I am ready to lend you a helping hand. You may fetch away the grey when you like. You will have to sign an acknowledgment, and promise to return her in good and sound condition. Always safest to have a contract properly executed and signed, then there can be no starting up of a misunderstanding afterwards.'

'I am to have your grey!' Oliver Luxmore could not believe in his good fortune, and this good fortune coming to him from such an unexpected quarter. 'There now! Honor said I was to go up to Langford and see you. She thought you might help, and 'twas no use in the world asking at Chimsworthy.'

'Honor said that!' exclaimed Taverner, and he looked at the girl and nodded approvingly.

Then Luxmore, who had been sitting in his shirt-sleeves, took his coat and put it on, went to the nail and unhooked his hat.

'I don't mind if I go and look at the grey,' he said. He had sufficient prudence not to accept till he had seen.

Whilst Oliver Luxmore was assuming his coat, Langford, leaning on his arms in the window, watched the active fingers of Honor, engaged in weaving a basket. Her feet were thrust forward, with the red stockings encasing them.

'Ah!' said Taverner, half aloud, half to himself; 'I know a red spider that brings luck. Well for him who secures her.'

Just then voices were audible, bright and clear, coming from the lane; and in a few minutes up the steps trooped the younger children of the carrier, returning from school. Each, even the boy of thirteen, went at once to Honor, stood before her, and showed face and hands and clothes.

'Please, Honor,' said one little girl, 'I've got a tear in my pinafore. I couldn't help it. There was a nail in the desk.'

'Well, Pattie, bring me my workbox.'

How clean, orderly, happy the children were! Each before going to school was examined to insure that it was scrupulously neat; and each on returning was submitted to examination again, to show that it had kept its clothes tidy whilst at school, and its face and hands clean.

Regardless of the presence and observations of Langford, Honor mended Pattie's pinafore. She was accustomed to do at once what she observed must be done. She never put off what had to be done to a future time. Perhaps this was one of the secrets of her getting through so much work.

When each child had thus reported itself to Honor, she dismissed it with a kiss, and sent it to salute the father.

'You will find, each of you, a piece of bread-and-butter and a mug of milk in the back kitchen,' she said. Then the children filed out of the room to where their simple meal was laid out for them.

'Busy, systematic, thrifty,' said Taverner Langford, looking approvingly at Honor. 'The three feet that stay Honour.' Whether he made this remark in reference to her name the girl could not make out; she looked up suddenly at him, but his face was inscrutable, as he stood with his back to the light in the window, with his broad-brimmed hat drawn over his eyes.

Her father was ready to depart with Langford. As the latter turned to go, he nodded to the girl in an approving and friendly way, and then turning to her father, as he prepared to descend the steps, said, 'What a maid that eldest daughter of yours is! Everything in your house is clean, everything in place, even the children. The sphere is not big enough for her, she has talents for managing a farm.'

'Ah!' groaned Luxmore, 'if we had our rights, and Coombe Park came to us——' The sisters heard no more. Their father had reached the foot of the steps.

When both he and Langford had disappeared, Kate burst out laughing.

'O Honor!' she said, 'that screw, Mr. Langford! how his voice creaked. I thought all the time he was speaking of a screw driven into father, creak, creak, creak!'

'For shame, Kate! Mr. Taverner Langford has done us a great kindness. He must not be ridiculed.'

'I do not believe in his kindness,' answered the lively Kate. 'The grey has got the glanders, or is spavined, that is why he wants to lend her. Unless father is very keen, Mr. Langford will overreach him.' Then she threw aside the basket she had been weaving. 'There, Honor, that is done, and my fingers are sore. I will do no more. No—not even to buy the grey with my earnings. I am sure that grey is coming to bring us ill-luck. I turned my thumb in all the time that Mr. Langford was here, I thought he had the evil eye, and—Honor— his wicked eye was on you.'

CHAPTER VI.

THE PROGRESS OF STRIFE.

So it fell out that two worthy men, land-owners, brothers-in-law, in the parish of Bratton Clovelly, each a churchwarden, each a pillar of religion, Jakim and Booz, one of the Temple, the other of the Tabernacle, were at variance. About what? About nothing, a little red spider, so minute that many a man could not see it without his spectacles.

The money-spinner had provoked the calling of names, the flying forth of fury, the rush of blood to the head of Hillary Nanspian, and a fit. It was leading to a good deal more, it was about to involve others beside the principals.

But the money-spinner was really only the red speck at the meeting-point of rivalries, and brooding discontents and growing grievances. Nanspian had long chafed at the superiority assumed by Langford, had been angry at his own ill-success, and envious of the prosperity of his brother-in-law. And Langford had fretted over the thriftlessness of Nanspian, and the prospect of his own gains being dissipated by his nephew.

Hillary was a boastful and violent man. Taverner was suspicious and morose. But Nanspian was good-natured at bottom; his anger, if boisterous, soon blew away. Langford's temper was bitter; he was not malevolent, but he harboured his wrongs, and made a sort of duty of revenging them.

The love of saving had become so much a part of Taverner's soul, that it caused him real agony of mind to think that all he had laid by might be wasted by young Hillary, who, brought up in his father's improvident ways, was sure to turn out a like wastrel. Moreover, he did not like young Larry. He bore him that curious aversion which old men sometimes manifest for the young. Taverner had been an ungainly youth, without ease of manner or social warmth. He had never made himself friends of either sex; always solitary, he had been driven in on himself. Now that he was in the decline of life he resented the presence in others of those qualities he had never himself possessed. The buoyant spirits, the self-confidence, the good humour, the pleasant looks, the swinging walk of young Larry were all annoyances to Langford, who would have taken a liking to the lad had he been shy and uncouth.

Formerly, scarcely a day had passed without the brothers-in-law meeting. Sometimes they encountered accidentally on Broadbury, or in the lanes, at other times they met by appointment at the Look-out Stone. They discussed together the weather, the crops, the cattle, the markets. Hillary was a shrewd man, and had seen more of the world than Taverner, who had, however, read more books than the other. Langford had respect for the worldly experience of his brother-in-law, and Nanspian venerated the book learning in the other. The Chimsworthy brother could see various ways in which money might be made, and had even made suggestions by which he of Langford had reaped a pecuniary profit, but he was too lazy a man to undertake new ventures himself, too lazy even to properly cultivate in the old way the land on which he lived.

Hillary was conscious that he was falling in the estimation of his brother-in-law. He was chafed by the sense of his indebtedness to him. He saw no way of escape from the debt he owed save by Taverner's death, and he began to have a lurking hope of release in that way. He was not stimulated to activity. 'What is the advantage of making a labour of life,' he asked—not of his brother-in-law—'when a man has a comfortable property, and another in reversion?'

The great day of all, on which the kindly relations of the brothers-in-law were brought forward and paraded before the parish, was on the feast day of Coryndon's Charity. Then Hillary Nanspian arrived arm-in-arm with Taverner Langford, Hillary in his badger-skin waistcoat with red lappets, Taverner in dark homespun, with black cravat and high collar. As they walked down the village every man touched his hat and every woman curtsied. When they came to a puddle, and puddles are common in the roads of Bratton Clovelly, then Hillary Nanspian would say, 'Take care, Taverner, lest you splash your polished boots and dark breeches.' Thereupon the brothers-in-law unlinked, walked round the puddle, and hooked together on the further side. At the dinner, which was attended by the Rector, who sat at the head and carved, the waywarden and the overseer, the landlord of the 'Ring of Bells,' where the dinner was held, and several of the principal farmers, ex-feoffees, or feoffees in prospective, speeches were made. Hillary, with a glass of rum-and-water and a spoon in it, stood up and spoke of his fellow-churchwarden and feoffee and brother-in-law in such a rich and warm speech, that, under the united influence of hot strong rum, and weak maudlin Christianity, and sound general good-fellowship, and goose and suet pudding, the tears rose into the eyes of the hearers, and their moral feelings were as elevated as if they had heard a sermon of Mr. Romaine.

After that, Taverner proposed the health of his co-feoffee and churchwarden in a nervous, hesitating speech, during which he shuffled with his feet on the floor, and his hands on the table, and became hot and moist, and almost cried—not with tender emotion, but with the sense of humiliation at his own inability to speak with fluency. But, of course, all present thought this agitation was due to the great affection he bore to his brother-in-law.

When Parson Robbins, the Rector, heard of the quarrel, he was like one thunderstruck. He could not believe it. 'Whatever shall I do? I shall have to take a side. Mercy on us, what times we live in, when I am forced to take a side!'

As to the farmers generally, they chuckled. Now at last there was a chance of one of them getting into Coryndon's Charity and getting a lease of the poor's lands.

Hillary Nanspian recovered from his fit, but the breach between the brothers-in-law was not healed. When he again appeared at market he was greatly changed. The apoplectic stroke, the blood-letting, the call in of the money owed to Langford, had combined to alter him. He was not as florid, as upright, as imperious as before. His face was mottled, the badger-skin waistcoat no longer fitted him as a glove, it fell into wrinkles, and the hair began to look as though the moth had got into it. A slight stoop appeared in his gait. He became querulous and touchy. Hitherto, when offended, he had discharged a big, mouth-filling oath, as a mortar throws a shell; now he fumed, and swore, and grumbled. There was no appeasing him. He was like the mitrailleuse that was to be, but was not then. Hitherto, he had sat on his settle, smoking, and eating his bread and cheese, and had allowed the fowls to come in and pick up the crumbs at his feet. Now he threw sticks at them and drove them out of the kitchen.

Encounters between the brothers-in-law were unavoidable, but when they met they pretended not to see each other. They made circuits to avoid meeting. When they passed in the lane, they looked over opposite hedges.

The quarrel might, perhaps, have been patched up, had it not been for the tongue of Mrs. Veale. Taverner Langford disliked this pasty-faced, bleached woman greatly, but he was afraid of dismissing her, because he doubted whether it would be possible for him to provide himself with as good a manager in his house and about the cattle. Though he disliked her, he was greatly influenced by her, and she found that her best mode of ingratiating herself with him was by setting him against others. She had a venomous dislike for the Nanspians. 'If anything were to happen to the master, those Nanspians would take all, and where should I be?' she reasoned. She thought her best chance of remaining at Langford and of insuring that something was left to her by the master in consideration for her faithful services was to make him suspect and dislike all who surrounded him. He listened to her, and though he discounted all she said, yet the repetition of her hints and suggestions, and retailed stories, told on him more than he allowed himself to believe. Through her he heard of the boasts of his brother-in-law, and his attention was called to fresh instances of mismanagement at Chimsworthy. At one time Mrs. Veale had audaciously hoped to become mistress of the place. Langford was a lone shy man, how could he resist the ambuscades and snares of a designing woman? But Mrs. Veale in time learned that her ambition in this direction was doomed to disappointment, and that efforts made to secure the master would effect her own expulsion. She therefore changed her tactics, dared to lecture and give him the rough of her tongue. Langford endured this, because it showed him she had no designs on him, and convinced him that she was severe and faithful. And she made herself indispensable to him in becoming the medium of communication between himself and those with whom he was offended. He had sufficient of the gentleman in him to shrink from reprimanding his servants and haggling with a dealer; he was miserly, but too much of a gentleman to show it openly. He made Mrs. Veale cut down expenses, watch against waste, and economise in small matters.

How is it that women are able to lay hold of and lead men by their noses as easily as they take up and turn about a teapot by its handle? Is it that their hands are fashioned for the purpose, and men's noses are fitted by Nature for their hands? Although the nose of Taverner Langford was Roman, and expressive of character and individuality, Mrs. Veale held him by it; and he followed with the docility of a colt caught and led by the forelock.

It was a cause of great disappointment to Hillary that Taverner was in a position to give him annoyance, whereas he was unable to retaliate. Langford had called in the money he had advanced to his brother-in-law; it must be repaid within three months. Langford had threatened the father and son with disinheritance. On the other side, he was powerless to punish Langford. The consciousness of this was a distress to Nanspian, and occasioned the irritability of temper we have mentioned. Unable to endure the humiliation of being hurt without being able to return the blow, he went into the office of the lawyer Physick, at Okehampton.

'Mr. Physick,' said he, 'I want to be thundering disagreeable.'

'By all means, Mr. Nanspian. Very right and proper.'

'I'm going to be very offensive.'

'To be sure. You have occasion, no question.'

'I want a summons made out against Mrs. Veale, that is, the housekeeper of Taverner Langford.'

'The deuce you do!' exclaimed the lawyer, starting into an erect position on his seat. 'The housekeeper of your brother-in-law!'

'The same. I want to hit him through her.'

'Why, Lord bless me! What has come to pass? I thought you and Mr. Langford were on the best of terms.'

'Then, sir, you thought wrong. We are no longer friends; we do not speak.'

'What has occasioned this?'

Nanspian looked down. He was ashamed to mention the red spider; so he made no reply.

'Well! and what is the summons to be made out for?'

'For giving me a stroke of the apoplexy.'

'I do not understand.'

'You must know,' said Hillary, lowering his voice, 'that I have a notion Mrs. Veale is a witch; and when Langford and I fell out she came meddling with her witchcraft. She came as a White Hare.'

'As a what?'

'As a White Hare,' answered Hillary, drawing forth a kerchief and blowing his nose, and in the act of blowing fixing the lawyer over the top of it with his eyes, and saying through it, 'My Larry saw her.'

Mr. Physick uttered a sigh of disappointment, and said ironically, 'This is not a case for me. You must consult the White Witch in Exeter.'

'Can you do nothing?'

'Certainly not. If that is all you have come about, you have come on a fool's errand.'

But this was not all. Nanspian wanted to raise the money for paying his brother-in-law. Mr. Physick was better able to accommodate him in this. 'There is another matter I want to know,' said Nanspian. 'Taverner Langford threatens to disinherit me and my Larry. Can he do it? I reckon not. You have the settlements. The threat is idle and vain as the wind, is it not?'

'Langford is settled property in tail male,' answered the solicitor. 'Should Mr. Langford die unmarried and without male issue, it will fall to you, and if you predecease, to your son.'

'There!' exclaimed Hillary, drawing a long breath, 'I knew as much; Larry and I are as sure of Langford as if we had our feet on it now. He cannot take it from us. We could, if we chose, raise money on it.'

'Not so fast, Mr. Nanspian. What aged man is your brother-in-law?'

'Oh, between fifty-eight and sixty.'

'He may marry.'

'Taverner marry!' exclaimed Hillary; he put his hands on his knees and laughed till he shook. 'Bless me! whom could Taverner marry but Mrs. Veale?—and he won't take her. He is not such a fool as to turn a servant under him into a mistress over him. But let him. I give him Mrs. Veale, and welcome. May I be at the wedding. Why, she will not see this side of forty, and there is no fear of a family.'

'He may take some one else.'

'She would not let him. She holds him under her thumb. Besides, there are none suitable about our neighbourhood. At Swaddledown are only children. Farmer Yelland's sister at Breazle is in a consumption, and at the rectory Miss Robbins is old. No, Mr. Physick, there is absolutely no one suitable for him.'

'Then he may take some one unsuitable.'

CHAPTER VII.

CORYNDON'S CHARITY.

The opinion gained ground in Bratton Clovelly that it was a pity two such good friends and worthy brothers-in-law should quarrel and be drawn on into acts of violence and vengeance, as seemed probable. As the Coryndon feoffee dinner drew on, expression was given to their opinion pretty freely, and the question was debated. What would happen at the dinner? Would the enemies refuse to meet each other? In that case, which would cede to the other? Perhaps, under the circumstance, the dinner would not take place, and the profits, not being consumed, would be given to the widows. That might establish a dangerous precedent. Widows in future years might quote this; and resist the reintroduction of the dinner. Fortunately widows, though often violent and noisy, are not dangerous animals, and may be browbeaten with impunity.

Nevertheless a general consensus of opinion existed among the overseers, and way-wardens, acting, ex-, and prospective, that the dinner must not be allowed to fall through even for one year. Englishmen, with their habitual caution, are very much afraid of establishing a precedent.

Hillary Nanspian was spoken to on the subject, and he opined that the dinner must be held. 'If Taverner Langford is ashamed to meet me, let him stay away. I shall pay him every penny I owed, and can look him in the face. We shall be merrier without him.'

Notice of the dinner was sent to Langford; he made no reply, but from his manner it was concluded that he would not attend.

The day of the Trust dinner arrived. Geese had been killed. Whiff! they could be smelt all down the village to leeward of the inn, and widows came out and sniffed up all they were likely to receive of Coryndon's Charity. Beef was being roasted. Hah! The eye that peeped into the kitchen saw it turning and browning before the great wood fire, and when the landlord's wife was not talking, the ear heard the frizzle of the fat and the drop, drop into the pan beneath.

What was that clinking? Men's hearts danced at the sound. A row of tumblers was placed on the dresser, and spoons set in them. In the dairy a maid was taking cream, golden as the buttercup, off the pans to be eaten—believe it, non-Devonians, if you can, gnash your teeth with envy and tear your hair—to be eaten with plum-pudding. See! yonder stands a glass vessel containing nutty-white celery in it, the leaves at the top not unfolded, not green, but of the colour of pale butter. Hard by is a plate with squares of cheese on it, hard by indeed, for, oh—what a falling off is there!—the Devon cheese is like board.

About the door of the 'Ring of Bells' was assembled a knot of men in their Sunday best, with glossy, soaped faces. They were discussing the quarrel between the brothers-in-law when the Rector arrived. He was a bland man, with a face like a suet-pudding; he shook hands cordially with every one.

'We've been talking, Parson, about the two who have got across. 'Tis a pity now, is it not?'

Parson Robbins looked from one to another, to gather the prevailing opinion, before he committed himself. Then, seeing one shake his head, and hearing another say, 'It's a bad job,' he ventured to say, 'Well, it may be so considered.' He was too cautious a man to say 'I consider it so;' he could always edge out of an 'It may be so considered.' Parson Robbins was the most inoffensive of men. He never, in the pulpit, insisted on a duty lest he should offend a Churchman, nor on a doctrine lest he should shock a Dissenter. It was his highest ambition to stand well with all men, and he endeavoured to gain his point by disagreeing with nobody and insisting on nothing.

'I hear,' said Farmer Yelland, 'that the two never meet each other and never speak. They are waiting a chance of flying at each other's throats.'

'Ah!' observed the Rector, 'so it has been reported in the parish.' He was too careful to say 'reported to *me*.'

'Why, pity on us!' said a little cattle-jobber with a squint; 'when folks who look straight before them fall across, how am I to keep straight with my eyes askew?'

49

Every one laughed at these words. Harry Piper, the speaker, was a general favourite, because his jokes were level with their comprehension, and he did not scruple to make a butt of himself. The sexton, a solemn man, with such command over his features that not a muscle twitched when a fly walked on his nose, even he unbent, and creases formed about his mouth.

'Now look here,' said Piper, 'if we don't take the matter in hand these two churchwardens will be doing each other a mischief. Let us reconcile them. A better day than this for the purpose cannot be found.'

'Mr. Piper's sentiments are eminently Christian,' said the Rector, looking round; then qualifying his statement with, 'that is, as far as I can judge without going further into the matter.'

'Will Master Nanspian be here?' asked one.

'I know that he will,' answered the cattle-jobber, 'but not the other, unless he be fetched.'

'Well, let him be fetched.'

'That is,' said the Parson, 'if he will come.'

There was then, leaning against the inn door, a ragged fellow with a wooden leg, and a stump of an arm into which a hook was screwed—a fellow with a roguish eye, a bald head, and a black full beard. Tom Crout lived on any little odd jobs given him by the farmers to keep him off the parish. He had lost his leg and arm through the explosion of a gun when out poaching. Now he drove bullocks to pasture, cows to be milked, sheep to the common, and wired rabbits. This was the proper man to send after Taverner Langford.

'You may ride my pony,' said the cattle-jobber, 'and so be quicker on your way.'

'And,' said the guardian of the poor, 'you shall dine on the leavings and drink the heel-taps for your trouble.'

As he went on his way, Crout turned over in his mind how he was to induce Taverner Langford to come to the dinner. Crout was unable to comprehend how any man needed persuasion to draw him to goose, beef, and plum-pudding.

On his way he passed Hillary Nanspian, in his badger-skin waistcoat with red lappets, riding his strawberry mare. He was on his way to the 'Ring of Bells.'

'Whither away, Crout?' shouted Hillary.

'Out to Broadbury, after Farmer Burneby's sheep that have broken.'

Then he rode on.

When he reached the gate of Langford, he descended. At once the black Newfoundland house-dog became furious, and flew at him, and with true instinct snapped at the calf of flesh, not the leg of wood. Tom Crout yelled and swore, and made the best of his way to the door, where Taverner and Mrs. Veale appeared to call off the dog.

'It is a shame to keep dogs like that, vicious brutes ready to tear a Christian to tatters.'

'I didn't suppose you was a Christian, hearing your heathenish oaths,' said Mrs. Veale; 'and as to the tatters, they were there before the dog touched you.'

'The parson has sent me,' said Crout, 'and he would not send me if I were not a Christian. As for my tatters, if you will give me an old coat, I'll leave them behind. Please, Mr. Langford, the feoffees and guests are at the "Ring of Bells," and cannot begin without you. The beef is getting cold, and the goose is becoming burnt.'

'Let them fall to. The dinner is sure to be good.'

'How can they, master, without you or Mr. Nanspian?'

'Is he not there?'

'Not a speck of his fur waistcoat visible, not a glimmer of his blue eye to be seen. Ah, Mr. Langford, such a dinner! Such goose, with onion stuffing, and sage, and mint, and marjoram! I heard the butcher tell our landlord he'd never cut such a sirloin in all his life as that roasting for to-day; smells like a beanfield, and brown as a chestnut! As for the plum-pudding, it is bursting with raisins!'

'That will suffice,' said Taverner, unmoved by the description. 'I do not intend to go.'

'Not intend to go! Very well, then, I shall have to go to Chimsworthy and bring Mr. Nanspian. I'll tell him you haven't the heart to meet folks. You prefer to hide your head here, as if you had committed something of which you are ashamed. Very well. When he hears that you durstn't show, he will go and swagger at the "Ring of Bells" without you.'

'I do not choose to meet him. He may be there after all.'

'Not a bit. When I left all were assembled, and he was not there. May I be struck dead if he was there! The parson said to the rest, "Whatever shall we do without Master Langford, my own churchwarden, so to speak—my right hand, and the representative of the oldest and grandest family in the place. That is a come-down of greatness if he don't turn up at the feoffees' dinner." May I die on the doorstep if these were not his very words! Then he went on, "I did reckon on Master Langford to be here to keep me in countenance. Now here I lay down my knife and fork, and not a bite will I eat, nor a cut will I make into that bubbling, frizzling, savoury goose, unless Taverner Langford be here. So go along, Crout, and fetch him."'

'Is that true?' asked Langford, flattered.

'May my remaining leg and arm wither if it be not! Then Farmer Burneby up and said, "He durstn't come, he's mortally afraid of meeting Hillary Nanspian."'

'Did he say that?' asked Taverner, flushing.

'Strike me blind if he did not!'

'I'll come. Go on, I will follow.'

When Crout returned to the 'Ring of Bells,' he found Nanspian there, large and red. The cripple slipped up to Piper and whispered, 'He'll be here, leave a place opposite the other, and fall to at the beef.'

'The fly,' observed the parson to a couple of farmers—'the fly is the great enemy of the turnip. It attacks the seed-leaves when they appear.'

'That is true.'

'Now, what you want with turnips is a good shower after the seed has been sown, and warmth to precipitate the growth at the critical period. At least, so I have been informed.'

'It is so, Parson.'

'In wet weather the fly does not appear, or the plant grows with sufficient rapidity to outstrip the ravages of the fly.'

'To be sure, you are quite right, sir.'

This fact of the turnip-fly was one of the few scraps of agricultural information Parson Robbins had picked up, and he retailed it at tithe, club, and feoffee dinners.

Then the landlord appeared at the inn door, and announced, 'All ready, gentlemen! sorry you have been kept waiting!'

At the moment that Nanspian and the parson entered, Langford arrived and went after them, without seeing the former, down the passage to the long room. The passage was narrow, tortuous, and dark. 'Wait a bit, gentlemen,' said the host, 'one at a time through the door; his Reverence won't say grace till all are seated.'

'Here is a place, Master Langford,' said Piper, 'on the right hand of the parson, with your back to the window. Go round his chair to get at it.'

Taverner took the place indicated. Then the Rector rapped on the table, and all rose for grace.

As Langford rose he looked in front of him, and saw the face of

Nanspian, who sat on the Rector's left. Hillary had not observed him before, he was looking at the goose. When he raised his eyes and met the stare of Taverner, his face became mottled, whereas that of his brother-in-law turned white. Neither spoke, but sank into his place, and during dinner looked neither to right, nor left, nor in front. Only once did Taverner slyly peep at Hillary, and in that glimpse he noted his altered appearance. Hillary was oldened, fallen away, changed altogether for the worse. Then he drew forth his blue cotton pocket-handkerchief and cleared his nose. Neither relished his dinner. The goose was burnt and flavourless, the beef raw and tough, the potatoes under-boiled, the apple-tart lacked cloves, the plum-pudding was over-spiced, the cheese was tough, and the celery gritty. So, at least, they seemed to these two, but to these two alone. When the spirits were produced all eyes were turned on Hillary Nanspian, but he neither rose nor spoke. Taverner Langford was also mute. 'Propose the health of the chairman,' whispered Piper into Hillary's ear.

'I am people's churchwarden,' answered he sullenly.

'Propose the health of the chairman,' said his right hand neighbour to Langford.

'I am a Dissenter,' he replied.

Then the Rector stood up and gave the health of the King, which was drunk with all honours.

'Shall we adjourn to the fire?' asked he; 'each take his glass and pipe.'

Then up rose the Rector once again, and said, 'Ahem! Fill your glasses, gentlemen. Mr. Langford, I insist. No shirking this toast. You, Mr. Nanspian, need no persuasion. Ahem!'

Piper came round and poured spirits into Langford's glass, then hot water.

'Ahem!' said the Rector. 'I have been in your midst, I may say, as your spiritual pastor, set—set—ahem!—under you these forty years, and, I thank heaven, never has there been a single discord—ahem!—between me and my parishioners. If I have not always been able to agree with them—ahem!—I have taken care not to disagree with them! I mean—I mean, if they have had their opinions, I have not always seen my way to accepting them, because I have studiously avoided having any opinions at all. Now—ahem!—I see a slight jar between my nearest and dearest neighbours,' he looked at Langford and Nanspian. 'And I long to see it ended.' ('Hear, hear, hear!') 'I express the unanimous opinion of the entire parish. On this one point, after forty opinionless years, I venture—ahem!—to have an opinion, a decided opinion, an emphatic opinion'—(immense applause)—'I call upon you all, my Christian brethren, to unite with me in healing this unseemly quarrel—I mean this quarrel: the unseemliness is in the quarrel, not in the quarrellers.'

Langford drank his gin-and-water not knowing what he did, and his hand shook. Nanspian emptied his glass. Both looked at the door: there was no escape that way, the back of burly Farmer Brendon filled it. All eyes were on them.

'Come now,' said Piper, 'what is the sense of this quarrel? Are you women to behave in this unreasonable manner? You, both of you, look the worse for the squabble. What is it all about?'

'Upon my word, I do not know,' said Nanspian. 'I never did Langford a hurt in my life. Why did he insult me?'

'I insult him!' repeated Taverner. 'Heaven knows I bore him no ill-will, but when he dared to address me as——'

'I swear by——' burst in Hillary.

'Do not swear!' said Langford, hastily. 'Let your yea be yea.' The ice was broken between them. One had addressed the other. Now they looked each other full in the face. Hillary's eyes moistened. Taverner's mouth twitched.

'Why did you employ offensive language towards me?' asked Hillary.

'I!' exclaimed Taverner; 'no, it was you who addressed me in words I could not endure.'

The critical moment had arrived. In another moment they would clasp hands, and be reconciled for life. No one spoke, all watched the two men eagerly.

'Well, Taverner,' said Hillary, 'you know I am a hot man, and my words fly from my tongue before I have cooled them.'

'I dare say I may have said what I never meant. Most certainly what I did say was not to be taken seriously.'

'But,' put in Parson Robbins, 'what *was* said?'

'Judge all,' exclaimed Taverner. 'I was angry, and I called Hillary Nanspian a long-tailed Cornish ourang-outang.'

The moment the words were uttered, he was aware that he had made a mistake. The insult was repeated in the most public possible manner. If the words spoken in private had exasperated Hillary, how much more so now!

Nanspian no sooner heard the offensive words than he roared forth, 'And I—I said then, and I repeat now, that you are nose-led, tongue-lashed by your housekeeper, Mrs. Veale.' Then he dashed his scalding rum-and-water in the face of his brother-in-law.

CHAPTER VIII.

A MALINGERER.

The time taken by the 'Vivid' over the journey to and from the market towns was something to be wondered at. A good man is merciful to his beast. Certainly Oliver Luxmore was a good man, and he showed it by his solicitude for the welfare of the grey. On Friday he drove to Tavistock market at a snail's pace, to spare the horse, because it had to make a journey on the morrow to Launceston or Okehampton. On Saturday he drove to market at a slug's pace, because the grey had done such hard work on the preceding day. The road, as has been said, was all up and down hill, and the hills are as steep as house roofs. Consequently the travellers by the 'Vivid' were expected to walk up the hills to ease the load, and to walk down the hills lest the weight of the 'Vivid' should carry the van over the grey. The fare one way was a shilling, the return journey could be made for sixpence. All goods, except what might be carried on the lap, were paid for extra. As the man said who was conveyed in a sedan-chair from which the bottom had fallen out, but for the honour of the thing, he might as well have walked. Passengers by the 'Vivid' started at half-past six in the morning, and reached the market town about half-past eleven. They took provisions with them, and ate two meals on the way. They also talked their very lungs out; but the recuperative power of their lungs was so great that they were fresh to talk all the way home. The van left the town at four and reached Bratton at or about nine.

A carrier must naturally be endowed with great patience. Oliver Luxmore was by nature thus qualified. He was easy-going, gentle, apathetic. Nothing excited him except the mention of Coombe Park. His business tended to make him more easy-going and patient than he was naturally. He allowed himself to be imposed upon, he resented nothing, he gave way before every man who had a rough, and every woman who had a sharp, tongue. He was cheerful and kindly. Every one liked him, and laughed at him.

One Saturday night, after his return from Okehampton, Oliver was taking his supper. The younger children were in bed, but Kate was up, she had been to market that day with her father. Kate was a very pretty girl, sharp eyed, sharp witted—with fair hair, a beautiful complexion, and eyes blue and sparkling—turquoises with the flash of the opal in them. She was seventeen. Her father rather spoiled her. He bought her ribbons and brooches when the money was needed for necessaries.

'I brought Larry Nanspian back part of the way with me,' said Oliver. 'His father drove him into town, but the old man stayed to drink, and Larry preferred to come on with me.'

'That was well of him,' said Honor, looking up with a smile.

'We talked of the grey,' continued the carrier. 'Larry was on the box with me. I put Kate inside, among the clucking, clacking old women. Larry asked me about the grey, and I told him how that we had got her. He shook his head, and he said, "Take care of yourself, Luxmore, lest in running out of the rain you get under the drip. I don't believe that Uncle Taverner is the man to do favours for nothing."'

'Did he say that?' asked Honor. 'He meant nothing by it—he was joking.'

'Of course he was joking. We joke a good deal together about one thing or another. He is grown a fine fellow. He came swinging up to me with his thumbs in his armholes and said, "Mr. Luxmore, Honor won't be able to withstand me in this waistcoat. She'll fall down and worship."'

'Did he say that?' asked Honor, and her brow flushed.

'Tush! you must not take his words as seriously meant. He had got a fine satin waistcoat to-day, figured with flowers. He pulled his coat open to show it me. I suppose he thought the satin waistcoat would draw you as a scarlet rag will attract rabbits.'

Honor turned the subject.

'What more did he say about Mr. Langford?'

'Oh, nothing particular. He told me he was sorry that his father could not spare us a horse, to keep us out of the clutches of his uncle Taverner. Then he laughed and said you had warned him not to run into debt, and yet had led the way yourself.'

'Run into debt, how?'

Oliver evaded an answer. 'In going up the hills, Kate and he walked together. He got impatient at last, and walked on by himself, and we never caught him up again.'

Honor did not look up from her work. She was mending some clothes of one of the children.

'He asked me a great deal about you,' said Kate. 'He said it was a shame that you should stick at home and never go to market, and see life.'

'How can I, with the house to look after? When you are a little more reliable, Kate, I may go. I cannot now.' Suddenly they heard a loud, deep voice at the door.

'Halloo! what a climb to the cock-loft.'

They looked startled to the door, and saw a man standing in it, with military trousers on his legs, and his hands in his pockets, watching them, with a laugh on his face.

'You have some supper! That's well. I'm cussed hungry. Walked from Tavistock. Why weren't you there to-day, father?'

'It is Charles!' exclaimed Luxmore, springing to his feet, and upsetting the table as he did so—that the cyder jug fell and was broken, and spilt its contents, and some plates went to pieces on the floor.

'Charlie, welcome home! Who would have expected to see you? Where have you been? What have you done? Have you served your time? Have you got your discharge? Lord, how glad I am to see you!'

Charles Luxmore, who entered the cottage, was a tall man, he looked ragged and wretched. His shoes were worn out, and his feet, stockingless, showed through the holes. His military trousers were sun-scorched, worn, badly patched, and in tatters about the ankles. His coat was split down the back, brown where exposed to the brunt of the weather. His whole appearance was such, that one who met him in a lonely lane would be sensible of relief when he had passed him, and found himself unmolested.

'Halloo! there,' said he, drawing near to the fallen table, picking up the broken jug, and swearing, because the last drops of cyder were out of it. 'What are you staring at me for, as if I were a wild beast escaped from a caravan? Curse me, body and bones, don't you know me?'

'Charles!' exclaimed Honor, 'you home, and in this condition?'

'Dash it! is that you, Honor? How you have shot up. And this you, Kate? Thunder! what a pair of pretty girls you are. Where are the rest of the panpipes? Let me see them, and get my greeting over. Lug them out of bed that I may see them. Curse it, I forget how many of them there are.'

'Seven, beside our two selves,' said Honor. 'Nine in all.'

'Let me see them. Confound it! It must be got over.'

'The rest are in bed,' said Honor. 'They must not be disturbed out of their sleep.'

'Never mind. Where is the old woman?'

'I do not know whom you mean, Charles.'

'Mother. Where is she?'

'Dead, Charles.'

He was silent for a moment. Then he said, 'Fetch the little devils, I want to see them.'

'Charles, for shame!' exclaimed Honor, reddening and frowning, and her brown eyes flashed an angry light.

'Tut, tut! soldier's talk. You won't find my tongue wear kid gloves. I meant no harm.'

'You shall not speak of the children in such terms,' said Honor, firmly.

'Halloo! Do you think I will stand being hectored by you?'

'There, there,' threw in Oliver Luxmore, 'the boy meant nothing by it. He has got into a careless way of expressing himself. That is all.'

'That is all,' laughed Charles, 'and now I have a true soldier's thirst, and I am not a dog to lap up the spilt liquor off the floor. What is it, beer? Is there any brandy in the house?'

'You can have a drop of cyder,' said Honor, with frowning brows. 'Or, if that does not please you, water from the spring. The cyder is middling, but the water is good.'

'No water for me. Fetch me the cyder.'

'There is a hogshead in the cellar under the stairs in the back kitchen,' said Honor. 'Fill yourself a mug of it.'

'You can fetch it for me.'

'I can do so, but I will not,' answered Honor. 'Charles, I will not stir hand or foot for a man who will speak of his innocent little brothers and sisters as you have done.'

'Take care of yourself!' exclaimed Charles, looking at her threateningly.

She was not overawed by his look. Her cheeks glowed with inner agitation. 'I am not afraid of you,' she said, and reseated herself at her work.

'I will fetch the cyder,' offered the good-natured Kate, springing into the back kitchen.

'That is a good, dear girl,' said Charles; 'you and I will be friends, and stand out against that dragon.'

He took the mug. 'Pshaw! this is not sufficient. I am thirsty as desert sand. Fetch me a jugful.'

'There is not another jug in the house,' said Kate. 'I will fill the mug again.'

Just then at the kitchen door appeared a white figure.

'Whom have we here?' exclaimed Charles.

'Joe! what has brought you down? Go to bed again,' said Honor.

'Not a bit; come here. I am the eldest in the house. I take the command by virtue of seniority,' shouted Charles, and springing from the chair, he caught the little white figure, brought the child in, and seated him on his knee. 'I am your brother,' said Charles. 'Mind this. From henceforth you obey me, and don't heed what Honor says.'

Honor looked at her father. Would he allow this? Oliver made no remark.

'What is your name, young jack-a-napes?' asked Charles, 'and what brings you here?'

'I am Joseph, that is Joe,' answered the little boy. 'I heard your voice, and something said about soldiers, and I crawled downstairs to see who you were.'

'Let the child go to bed,' asked the father. 'He will catch a chill in his nightshirt.'

'Not he,' replied Charles. 'The kid wants to hear what I have to say, and you are all on pins, I know.'

'Well, that is true,' said Oliver Luxmore. 'I shall be glad to learn what brings you home. You have not served your full time. You have not bought yourself out. If you were on leave, you would be in uniform.'

'Oh, I'm out of the service,' answered Charles. 'Look here.' He held out his right hand. The forefinger was gone. 'I cut it off myself, because I was sick of serving his Majesty, tired of war and its hardships. I felt such an inextinguishable longing for home, that I cut off my trigger finger to obtain my discharge.'

'For shame, Charles, for shame!' exclaimed Honor.

'Oh? you are again rebuking me! You have missed your proper place. You should be army chaplain. I've been in India, and I've fought the Afghans. Ah! I've been with General Pollock, and stormed and looted Cabul.'

'You have been in battle!' exclaimed little Joe.

'I have, and shot men, and run my bayonet into a dozen naked Afghans.' He laughed boisterously. 'It is like sticking a pig. That sack of Cabul was high fun. No quarter given. We blew up the great bazaar, crack! boom! high into the air, but not till we had cleared away all the loot we could. And, will you believe it? we marched away in triumph, carrying off the cedar doors of Somnath, as Samson with the gates of Gaza. Lord Ellenborough ordered it, and we did it. But they were not the original gates after all, but copies. Then, damn it, I thought——'

'Silence,' said Honor indignantly. 'With the child on your knee will you curse and swear?'

'An oath will do no harm, will it, Joe?' asked the soldier, addressing the little boy, who sat staring in his face with wonder and admiration. 'A good oath clears the heart, as a cough relieves a choking throat, is it not so, Joe? or as a discharge of guns breaks a waterspout, eh?' The little boy looked from his brother to his sister. It was characteristic of the condition of affairs in the house that he did not look to his father.

'I don't know, brother Charles,' answered he. 'Honor would not allow it, she says it is wicked.'

'Oh, she!' mocked the soldier. 'I suppose you are under petticoat government still, or have been. Never mind, Joe. Now that I am come home

63

you shall take orders from me, and not from her.'

'Joe,' said Honor sternly, 'go at once to bed.'

'He shall stay and hear the rest of the story. He shall hear how I lost my finger.'

The child hesitated.

Then Honor said gravely, 'Joe, you will do that which you know to be right.'

At once the little boy slipped from his brother's knee, ran to Honor, threw his arms round her neck, kissed her on both cheeks, and ran away, upstairs.

'So, so,' said Charles, 'open war between us! Well, sister, you have begun early. We shall see who will obtain the victory.'

'I don't think Honor need fear a soldier who cuts off his finger to escape fighting,' said Kate.

'What, you also in arms against me?' exclaimed Charles, turning on the younger sister.

'You asked Joe if he were under petticoat government, and sneered at him for it; but you seem to be valiant only when fighting petticoats,' retorted Kate.

'I'm in a wasp's nest here,' laughed Charles.

'Never mind Kate,' said Oliver, 'she has a sharp tongue. Tell us further about your finger.'

'I lost more than my finger—I lost prize money and a pension. As I told you, I was weary of the service, and wanted to get home. I thought I should do well with all the loot and prize-money, and if I were wounded also and incapacitated for service, I should have a pension as well; so I took off my finger with an axe, and tried to make believe I was hurt in action. But the surgeon would not allow it. I got into trouble and was discharged with the loss of my prize-money as a malingerer.'

'You are not ashamed to tell us this?' exclaimed Honor.

'It was a mistake,' said Charles.

'We are ashamed to sit and listen to you,' said Honor, with an indignant flash of her eyes, and with set brows. 'Come, Kate, let us to bed and leave him.'

'Good night, malingerer,' said Kate.

CHAPTER IX.

CHARLES LUXMORE.

The next day was Sunday. Charles lay in bed, and did not appear to breakfast. Oliver Luxmore, Kate, and the younger children were dressed for church. Honor remained at home alternately with Kate on Sunday mornings to take care of Tempie, the youngest, and to cook the dinner. This was Honor's morning at home.

Oliver Luxmore stood in doubt, one moment taking his Sunday hat, then putting it back in its card box, then again changing his mind.

Before they started, Charles swaggered into the kitchen, and asked for something to eat.

'Where are you all going to, you crabs, as gay as if fresh scalded?' asked Charles.

'This is Sunday,' answered his father, 'and I was thinking of taking them to church; but if you wish it, I will remain at home.'

'Suit yourself,' said Charles, contemptuously, 'only don't ask me to go with you. I should hardly do you credit in these rags, and the parson would hardly do me good. In India there were four or five religions, and where there is such a choice one learns to shift without any.'

'What had I better do?' asked Oliver turning to Honor.

'Go to church with the children, father. I will remain with Charles.'

'I am to have your society, am I?' asked the soldier. 'An hour and a half of curry, piping hot! Well, I can endure it. I can give as well as take. Let me have a look at you, Kate. A tidy wench, who will soon be turning the heads of the boys, spinning them like tee-totums. Let me see your tongue.' Kate put out her tongue, then he chucked her under the chin and made her bite her tongue. The tears came into her eyes.

'Charles! you have hurt me. You have hurt me very much.'

'Glad to hear it,' he said, contemptuously. 'I intended to do it. The tongue is too long, and too sharp, and demands clipping and blunting. I have chastised you for your impertinence last night.'

'I suppose I had better go,' said Oliver.

'Certainly, father,' answered Honor.

Then, still hesitating at every step from the cottage to the lane, Oliver went forth followed by seven children.

Charles drew a short black pipe from his pocket, stuffed it with tobacco, which he carried loose about him, and after lighting it at the fire on the hearth, seated himself in his father's chair, and began to smoke. Presently he drew the pipe out of his mouth, and looking askance at his sister, said 'Am I to forage for myself this morning?'

Honor came quietly up to him, and standing before him, said, 'I spoke harshly to you, Charles, last night. I was angry, when you talked of the dear little ones offensively. But I dare say you meant no harm. It is a bad sign when the words come faster from the lips than the thoughts form in the heart. You shall have your breakfast. I will lay it for you on the table. I am afraid,

66

Charles, that your service in the army has taught you all the vices and none of the virtues of the soldier. A soldier is tidy and trim, and you are dirty and ragged. I am sorry for you; you are my brother, and I have always loved you.'

'Blazes and fury!' exclaimed Charles; 'this is a new-fangled fashion of showing love. I have been from home five years, and this is the way in which I am welcomed home! I have come home with a ragged coat, and therefore I am served with cold comfort. If I had returned with gold guineas I should have been overwhelmed with affection.'

'Not so,' said Honor gravely. 'If you had returned with a sound character we would respect the rags; but what makes my heart ache is to see, not the tattered jacket, but the conscience all to pieces. How long is it since you landed?'

'Five or six months ago.'

'Where have you been since your return?'

'Where I could spend my money. I did bring something with me, and I lived on it whilst it lasted. It is not all gone yet. Look here.' He plunged his hand into his trousers pocket and jingled his coins carelessly in it.

'There!' said he, 'you will feel more respect for me, and your love wake up, when you see I have money still, not much, but still, some. Curse it, I was a fool not to buy you a ribbon or a kerchief, and then you would have received me with smiles instead of frowns.'

Honor looked him steadily in the face, out of her clear hazel eyes. 'No, Charles, I want no presents from you. Why did not you return to us at once?'

'Because I had no wish to be buried alive in Bratton Clovelly. Are you satisfied? Here I am at last.'

'Yes,' she repeated, 'here you are at last. What are you going to do now you are here?'

'I don't know,' answered her brother with a shrug. Then he folded his arms, threw out his legs, and leaned back in the chair. 'A fellow like me, who

67

has seen the world, can always pick up a living.'

Honor sighed. What had he learned? For what was he fitted?

'Charles,' she said, 'this is your father's house, and here you were born. You have as true a right to shelter in it as I. You are heartily welcome, you may believe that. But look about you. We are not in Coombe Park. Including you we make up twelve in this cottage. What we live on is what your father earns by his carrying; but he is in debt, and we have no money to spare, we cannot afford to maintain idlers.'

'Take my money,' said Charles, emptying his pocket oh the table.

'No,' answered Honor. 'For a week we will feed you for nothing. That money must be spent in dressing you respectably. By next week you will have found work.'

'Maybe,' said the soldier. 'It is not every sort of work that will suit me. Any one want a gamekeeper about here?'

'No, Charles, there is only Squire Impey in this parish; besides, without your forefinger, who would take you as a gamekeeper?'

'The devil take me. I forgot that.'

'Curses again,' said Honor. 'You must refrain your mouth before the children.'

'I have not gone to church,' said Charles sullenly, 'because I didn't want to be preached to; spare me a sermon at home.'

'Charles,' said Honor, 'I have hard work to make both ends meet, and to keep the children in order. You must not make my work harder—perhaps impossible. If you remain here, you will need my help to make you comfortable and to put your clothes in order. You will throw an additional burden on me, already heavily weighted. I do not grudge you that. But remember that extra work for an additional member means less time for earning money at basket-weaving. We must come to an understanding. I do not grudge you the time or the trouble, but I will only give them to you on

68

condition that you do not interfere with my management of the children, and that you refrain your tongue from oaths and unseemly speech.'

Charles stood up, went to her, took her by both ears, and kissed her. 'There, corporal, that is settled.'

Honor resented the impertinence of laying hold of her by both ears, but she swallowed her annoyance, and accepted the reconciliation.

'I have a good heart,' said Charles, 'but it has been rolled in the mud.'

'Give us the goodness, and wash off the soil,' answered Honor. Then she brought him some bread-and-butter and milk. 'Charles,' she said, 'I will see if I cannot find some of father's clothes that will fit you. I cannot endure to see you in this condition.'

'Not suitable to the heir of Coombe Park, is it?' laughed Charles. 'Is the governor as mad on that now as of old?'

'Say nothing to him about Coombe Park, I pray you,' urged Honor. 'It takes the nerve out of his arms and the marrow from his bones. It may be that we have gentle blood in us, or it may not. I have heard tell that in old times servants in a house took the names of their masters.'

'I have always boasted I was a gentleman, till I came to believe it,' said the soldier. 'You'd have laughed to hear me talk of Coombe Park, and the deer there, and the coaches and horses, and father as Justice of Peace, and Deputy-Lieutenant, and all that sort of thing, and his wrath at my enlisting as a private.'

'I should not have laughed. I should have cried.'

'And, Honor, I reckon it is the gentle blood in my veins which has made a wastrel of me. I could never keep my money, I threw it away like a lord.'

Honor sighed. The myth of descent from the Luxmores of Coombe Park had marred her father's moral strength, and depraved her brother's character.

'There they come, the little devils!' shouted Charles, springing up and knocking the ashes out of his pipe, which he put away in his waistcoat pocket.

'Charles!' again remonstrated Honor, but in vain. Her elder brother was unaccustomed to control his tongue. There was a certain amount of good nature in him, inherited from his father, and this Honor thankfully recognised; but he was like his father run to seed. Luxmore would have become the same but for the strong sustaining character of his daughter.

Charley went to the door, and stood at the head of the steps. Along the lane came Oliver Luxmore with his children, Hillary junior and Kate bringing up the rear.

'Now then, you kids, big and little!' shouted Charles, 'see what I have got. A handful of halfpence. Scramble for them. Who gets most buys most sweeties.' Then he threw the coppers down among the children. The little ones held up their hands, jumped, tumbled over each other, quarrelled, tore and dirtied their Sunday clothes, whilst Charles stood above laughing and applauding. Oliver Luxmore said nothing.

'Come in, come in at once!' cried Honor, rushing to the door with angry face. 'Charles, is this the way you keep your promises?'

'I must give the children something, and amuse myself as well,' said the soldier.

Honor looked down the road and saw Kate with young Hillary Nanspian. They were laughing together.

'There now,' said Kate, as she reached the foot of the steps, 'Honor, see the young fellow who boasts he will make you fall down and worship his waistcoat.'

'It was a joke,' said Larry, turning red. He poked his hat up from his right, then from his left ear, he was overcome with shame.

Honor's colour slightly changed at the words of her sister, but she rapidly recovered herself.

'So,' continued the mischievous Kate, 'you have come round all this way

70

to blaze your new waistcoat in the eyes of Honor, because she could not come to church to worship it?'

Young Nanspian looked up furtively at Honor, ashamed to say a word in self-exculpation.

'Talk of girls giving themselves airs over their fine clothes!' said Kate, 'men are as proud as peacocks when they put on spring plumage.'

'It serves you right, Mr. Larry,' said Honor, 'that Kate torments you. Vanity must be humbled.'

'I spoke in jest,' explained Hillary. 'All the parish knows that when I joke I do not mean what I say. When a word comes to my lips, out it flies, good or bad. All the world knows that.'

'All the world knows that,' she repeated. 'It is bad to wear no drag on the tongue, but let it run down hill to a smash. Instead of boasting of this you should be ashamed of it.'

'I am not boasting,' he said, with a little irritation.

'Then I misunderstood you. When a man has a fault, let him master it, and not excuse himself with the miserable reason, that his fault is known to all the world.'

'Come, Honor, do not be cross with me,' he said, running up the steps, and holding out his hand.

'I am not cross with you,' she answered, but she did not give him her hand.

'How can I know that, if you will not shake hands?'

'Because all the world knows I tell no lies,' she answered coldly, and turned away.

CHAPTER X.

ON THE STEPS.

For a week Charles Luxmore made a pretence of looking for work. Work of various kind was offered him, but none was sufficiently to his taste for him to accept it. He had still money in his pocket. He did not renew his offer of it to Honor. She had fitted him in a suit of his father's clothes, and he looked respectable. He was often in the 'Ring of Bells,' or at a public-house in a neighbouring parish. He was an amusing companion to the young men who met in the tavern to drink. He had plenty to say for himself, had seen a great deal of life, and had been to the other side of the world. Thus he associated with the least respectable, both old and young, the drunkards and the disorderly.

He was not afflicted with bashfulness, nor nice about truth, and over his ale he boasted of what he had seen and done in India. He said no more about his self-inflicted wound; and was loud in his declamation against the injustice of his officers, and the ingratitude of his country which cast him adrift, a maimed man, without compensation and pension. When he had drunk he was noisy and quarrelsome; and those who sat with him about the tavern table were cautious not to fall into dispute with him. There was a fire in his eye which led them to shirk a quarrel.

About a mile from the church in a new house lived a certain Squire Impey, a gentleman who had bought a property there, but who did not belong to those parts. No one knew exactly whence he came. He was a jovial man, who kept hounds, hunted and drank. Charles went to him, and he was the only man for whom he condescended to do some work, and from whom to take pay; but the work was occasional, Charles was an amusing man to talk to, and Impey liked to have a chat with him. Then he rambled away to Coombe Park, where he made himself so disagreeable by his insolence, that he was ordered off the premises. His father and brothers and sisters did not see much of him;

he returned home occasionally to sleep, and when the mind took him to go to market, he went in the van with his father.

Much was said in the place of the conduct of Charles Luxmore—more, a great deal, than came to the ears of Honor. Oliver heard everything, for in the van the parish was discussed on the journey to market, and those who sat within did not consider whether the driver on the box heard what they said. Oliver never repeated these things to his eldest daughter, but Honor knew quite enough of the proceedings of Charles without this. She spoke to Charles himself, rebuked him, remonstrated with him, entreated him with tears in her eyes to be more steady; but she only made matters worse; she angered him the more because he knew that she was right. He scoffed at her anxiety about himself; he swore and burst into paroxysms of fury when she reprimanded him.

'Do not you suppose,' said he, 'that I am going to be brought under your thumb, like father and the rest.'

Possibly she might have been more successful had she gone to work more gently. But with her clear understanding she supposed that every one else could be governed by reason, and she appealed to his sense, not to his heart. He must see, she argued, to what end this disorderly life would lead, if she put it before him nakedly. She supposed she could prove to him her sisterly affection in no truer way than by rebuke and advice.

Although Honor's heart was full of womanly tenderness, there was something masculine in her character. There could not fail to be. Since her mother's death she had been the strength of the house, to her all had held. Circumstances had given her a hardness which was not natural to her.

Charles vowed after each fresh contest with Honor that he could not go near the cottage again. He would go elsewhere, out of range of her guns; but he did not keep his vow. It was forgotten on the morrow. Honor was not a scold. She had too good judgment to go on rebuking and grumbling, but she spoke her mind once, and acted with decision. She withstood Charles whenever his inconsiderate good nature or his disorderly conduct threatened to disturb the clocklike working of the house, to upset the confidence the children had in her, and to mar their simplicity. She encountered his violence with fearlessness. She never became angry, and returned words for words, but she held to her decision with toughness. Her father was afraid of Charles, and counselled his daughter to yield. Opposition, he argued, was unavailing, and would aggravate unpleasantnesses.

Honor suffered more than transpired. Her brother's disrepute rankled in her heart. She was a proud girl, and though she placed no store on her father's dreams of Coombe Park, she had a strong sense of family dignity, and she was cut to the quick when Charles's conduct became the talk of the neighbourhood. Never a talker, she grew more than ever reserved. When she went to or returned from church on Sunday, she shunned acquaintances; she would not linger for a gossip in the churchyard, or join company with a neighbour in the lane. She took a child by each hand, and with set face, and brows sternly contracted, looking neither right nor left, she went her way. Brightness had faded from her face. She was too proud to show the humiliation she felt at heart. 'Oh my,' said the urchins, 'bain't Red Spider mighty stuck up! Too proud to speak to nobody, now, seeming.'

Honor saw little of young Larry. Once or twice he made as though he would walk home with her from church, but she gave him no encouragement; she held little Charity's hand, and made Charity hold that of Martha, and kept Charity and Martha between her and the young man, breaking all familiar converse. She had not the heart to talk to him.

'You need not take on about Charles,' said her father one day. 'Every one knows that you are a good girl, and makes allowances for a soldier.'

'Disorderly ways,' answered Honor, 'are like infectious diseases. When one has an attack, it runs through the house.'

'Why do you not encourage folk to be friendly? You hold yourself aloof from all.'

Honor sighed.

'I cannot forget Charles, and the shame he is bringing on us. For me it matters little, but it matters much to the rest. The children will lose sense of fear at bad language, lies and bragging. Kate is a pretty girl, and some decent lad may take a fancy to her; but who would make a maid his wife who had such a brother?'

'Oh! as for that, young Larry Nanspian is after her. You should see how they go on together, tormenting and joking each other.'

Honor coloured and turned her face aside. She said nothing for a minute, then with composed voice and manner she went on.

'See the bad example set to Joe. He tries his wings to fly away from me, as is natural; boys resist being controlled by the apron. He sees his elder brother, he hears him, he copies him, and he will follow him down the road to destruction. We must get Joe away into service unless we can make Charles go, which would be the better plan of the two.'

'Charles has been away for some years. We must not drive him out of the house now we have him home again.'

'Father, I wish you would be firm with him.'

'I—I!' he shook his head, 'I cannot be hard with the boy. Remember what he has gone through in India, in the wars. Look at his poor hand. Home is a place to which a child returns when no other house is open to it.'

Honor looked sadly at the carrier. No help was to be had from him.

'I suppose, father,' she said, 'that there are rights all round. If Charles comes home claiming the shelter of our roof and a place at our table, he is bound in some way. He has no right to dishonour the roof and disturb the table. I grudge him no pains to make him comfortable, but I do expect he will not make it impossible for me to keep the home decent.'

'Of course, of course, Honor,' said the carrier, rubbing his palms slowly between his knees, and looking vacantly into the fire. 'That is reasonable.'

'And right,' Honor. 'And, father, you should make a stand. Now, all the responsibility falls on me.'

'Oh, yes. I will make a stand; certainly, certainly,' said Luxmore. 'Now let us change the subject.'

'No,' the girl. 'I cannot, and I will not. Charles must be made to conduct himself properly. I will not allow the little ones to hear his profane talk, see his devil-may-care ways. Mother committed them to me, and I will stand between them and evil. If it comes to a fight, we shall fight. All I wish is that the fight not to be between brother and sister.' Her voice became hard, her brows contracted, her face became pale with intensity of feeling.

'There, there!' groaned Oliver Luxmore, 'don't make out matters worse they are. A sheep looks as big as a cow in a fog. You see ghosts where I see thorn-trees. Be gentler with Charles, not so peremptory. Men will not be ordered about by women. Charles is not a bad boy. There is meat on a trout as well as bones. All will come right in the end.'

Honor said no more. Her eyes filled; she stooped over her needlework to conceal them; her hand moved quickly, but the stitches were uneven.

'I will do something, I will indeed,' said Luxmore, rising. He took his hat and went out, but returned quickly a few minutes later, agitated, and went through the room, saying hastily, 'Honor! he is coming, and—I think—drunk.'

Then he escaped into the back kitchen and out into the paddock in the rear where he kept his horse. That was all the help Honor was likely to get from him—to be forewarned.

Next moment two of the children flew up the steps frightened and heated.

'O, Honor! Charlie is tight!'

Honor stood up, folded her needlework, put it aside, and went to the door.

'Children,' she said, 'go behind into the field to father.' Then she went to the head of the steps and looked down the lane.

She saw her brother, coming on with a lurching walk, holding a stick, followed by a swarm of school-children, recently dismissed, who jeered, pelted him, and when he turned to threaten, dispersed to gather again and continue tormenting. Charles was not thoroughly drunk, but he was not sober. Honor's brow became blood-red for a moment, and her hand trembled on the rail; but the colour left her forehead again, and her hand was firm as she descended the steps.

At the sight of Honor Luxmore the children fell back, and ceased from their molestations.

'Halloa, Honor!' shouted Charles, staggering to the foot of the steps. 'A parcel of gadflies, all buzz and sting! I'll teach 'em to touch a soldier! Let me pass, Honor, and get away from the creatures.'

'No, Charles,' answered his sister, 'you do not pass.'

'Why not?'

'Because I will not let you—drunk.'

'I am not drunk, not at all. It is you who are in liquor. Let me pass.' He put his hand on the rail, and took a step up.

'You shall not pass!' she spoke coolly, resolutely.

'Curse you for a pig-headed fool,' said Charles, 'I'm not going to be stopped by such as you.'

'Such as I shall stop you,' answered Honor. 'Shame on you to dishonour the steps by which our mother went down to her burial! Verily, I saw her in my dreams, putting her hands over her face in her grave to hide the sight of her son.'

'Stand aside.'

'I will not budge!'

'I was a fool to come home,' muttered Charles, 'to be pickled in vinegar like walnuts. I wish I'd stayed away.'

'I wish you had, Charles, till you had learned to conduct yourself with decency.'

'I will not be preached to,' he growled; then becoming lachrymose, he said, 'I come home after having been away, a wanderer, for many years. I come home from bloody wars, covered with wounds, and find all against me. This is a heartless world. I did expect to find love at home, and pity from my sister.'

'I love and pity you,' said Honor, 'but I can only respect him who is respectable.'

'Let me pass!

'I will not, Charles.'

Then he laid hold of her, and tried to pull her off the steps; but she had a firm grip of the rail, and she was strong.

The children in the lane, seeing the scuffle, drew near and watched with mischievous delight. Charles was not so tipsy that he did not know what he was about, not so far gone as to be easily shaken off. Honor was obliged to hold with both hands to the rail. He caught her round the waist, and slung her from side to side, whilst oaths poured from his lips. In the struggle her hair broke loose, and fell about her shoulders.

She set her teeth and her eyes glittered. Fire flamed in her cheeks. She was resolved at all costs not to let him go by. She had threatened that she would fight him, and now, before she had expected it, the fight was forced upon her.

Finding himself foiled, unable to dislodge her, and unable to pass her, Charles let go, went down the steps, and kicked and thrust at the support of the handrail, till he broke it down. Then, with a laugh of defiance, he sprang up the steps brandishing the post. But, when the rail gave way, Honor seized it, and ascending before him, facing him, stepping backward, she planted herself against the cottage door, with the rail athwart it, behind her, held with both hands, blocking the entrance.

Charles was forced to stay himself with the broken post he held, as he ascended the steps.

'Honor!' he shouted, 'get out of the way at once, I am dangerous when opposed.'

'Not to me,' she answered; 'I am not afraid of you, drunk or sober. You shall not cross this doorstep.'

He stood eyeing her, with the post half raised, threateningly. She met his unsteady gaze without flinching. Was there no one to see her there but the tipsy Charles and the frightened children? A pity if there was not. She was erect, dignified, with bosom expanded, as her bare arms were behind her. Her cheeks were brilliant with colour, her fallen hair, raining about her shoulders, blazed with the reel evening sun on it, her large hazel eyes were also full of fire. Her bosom heaved as she breathed fast and hard. She wore a pale, faded print dress, and a white apron. Below, her red ankles and feet were planted firm as iron on the sacred doorstep of Home, that she protected.

As Charles stood irresolute, opposite her, the children in the lane, thinking he was about to strike her, began to scream.

In a moment Hillary Nanspian appeared, sprang up the steps, caught Charles by the shoulder, struck the post out of his hand, and dragging him down the steps, flung him his length in the road.

'Lie there, you drunken blackguard!' he said; 'you shall not stand up till you have begged your sister's pardon, and asked permission to sleep off your drink in the stable.'

CHAPTER XI.

IN THE LINNEY.

Next morning, when Charles Luxmore awoke, he found himself lying on the hay in the little 'linney,' or lean-to shed, of his father. The door was open and the sun streamed in, intense and glaring. In the doorway, on a bundle of straw, sat his sister Honor, knitting. The sun was shining in and through her golden hair, and the strong, fiery light shone through her hands, and nose, and lips, crimson—or seemed to do so. Charles watched her for some time out of his half-closed eyes, and confessed to himself that she was a fine, noble-looking girl, a girl for a brother to be proud of. Her profile was to the light, the nose straight, the lips sharp-cut, now expanded, then closed tight, as moved by her thoughts, and her hair shone like the morning clouds above the rising sun.

'What! sentinel, keeping guard?' shouted Charles, stretching his limbs and sitting up. 'In custody, am I? Eh?'

'I have brought you your breakfast, Charles,' answered Honor. 'There is a bowl of bread and milk at your elbow.'

He was hungry, so he took the bowl. His hair was ruffled, and full of strands of hay; he passed his hand over his face.

'I've had many a sleep in a barn before now,' he said; 'there are worse bedrooms, but there is one drawback. You can't smoke a pipe in one, or you run the chance of setting fire to bed and house. I did that once, and had a near scratch to escape before the flames roasted me. Best was, I managed to escape before any one was on the spot, so I was not taken up; suspicion fell on a labourer who had been dismissed a fortnight before.'

'And you said nothing?'

'Certainly not. Do you take me for a fool?'

Honor's lips contracted, so did her brow.

Charles put the spoon into the bread and milk, then, as he was setting it to his mouth, burst out laughing, and spilt the sop over his clothes.

'It was enough to make a fellow laugh,' he explained. 'To see last night how scared the kids were—Martha and Charity—and how they cut along when they saw me coming home.'

'This is not a cause for laughter. If you had a heart you would weep.'

'I thought I caught sight of father.'

'You did, but he also turned and left you. He could not face you as you were. You should be ashamed of yourself, Charles.'

'There, there!' he exclaimed impatiently, 'I will listen to no rebukes. I was not drunk, only a bit fresh.'

'Drunk or fresh matters little, you were not in a fit condition to come home; and what is more, I will not allow you to live in this cottage longer.'

'You will not?'

'No, I will not.'

'Who is to prevent me?'

'I will.'

'You!—and what if I force you out of the way, and go in and brave you?'

'You may go in, but I leave and take with me all the little ones. I have made up my mind what to do; I can work and earn enough to support the children, but I will not—no, I will not let them see you and hear you more.'

He looked at her. Her face was resolute. She was the girl to carry out her threat.

'I curse the day I came back to see your wry face,' he muttered, and rolled over on his side, away from her.

She made no reply. Her lips quivered. He did not see it, as he was no longer looking at the door.

'Home is home,' he said, 'and go where one will there are threads that draw one back to it.'

Honor was softened. 'I am glad, Charles, that you love home. If you love it, respect it.'

'Don't fancy that I came home out of love for you.'

Honor sighed.

'I came home to see how father fared about Coombe Park, and how mother was flourishing.'

'Well, Charles, I am glad you thought of father and mother. You must have a right heart, at ground. Mother is dead, but I know she shames over your bad conduct, and would rejoice were you to mend.'

'How do you know that? There is no postal communication with the other world, that I am aware of.'

'Never mind how I know it, but I do.'

'I was a fool to return. There is no kindness left in the world. If there were I should find a pinch at home, and pity from you.'

'Charles, if I have been harsh with you, it has been through your own fault. God, who reads all hearts, knows that I love you. But then, I love all the rest of my brothers and sisters, and now that mother is not here to see after them, whom have they got but myself to protect them? I defend them as a cat defends her kittens from a dog. Charles, I am sorry if I have been rough and unkind, and unsisterly to you, but indeed, indeed I cannot help myself. Mother laid the duty on me when she was dying. She caught my hand—so,' she grasped his wrist, and looking earnestly in his face, said, 'and laid it on

82

me to be father and mother to the little ones. I bent over her and kissed her, and promised I would, and she died with her hand still holding my wrist. I feel her grip there to this day, whenever danger threatens the children. When you first came into the house, on your return, I felt her fingers close as tight on me as when she died. She is always with me, keeping me up to my duty. I cannot help myself, Charles; I must do what I know I ought, and I am sure it is wrong for me to allow you to remain with us longer. Consider, Charles, what the life is that you are now leading.'

'The life is all right,' said he moodily. 'I can pay my way. I have more brains than any of these clodhoppers round, and can always earn my livelihood.'

'Begin about it,' urged Honor.

'Time enough for that when the last copper is gone wherewith to stop a pipe and fill a can of ale.'

'O Charles! Charles!' exclaimed his sister, 'your own coppers are spent long ago. Now you are smoking the clothes off your little brothers' and sisters' backs, and drinking and squandering the little money I have for feeding them. For shame!' the blood rushed into her cheeks with sudden anger, as the injustice of his conduct presented itself before her vividly. 'Your father works that you may idle! It is a shame! It is a sin.'

'Hold your tongue!'

'I will not hold my tongue,' she answered hotly. 'You know how good, and gentle, and forbearing father is, how ready he is to give everything to his children, how unwilling to say to any one a harsh word, and you take advantage of his good nature; you, that should be building up the house, are tearing it down on the heads of all of us, father, Kate, Patience, Joe, Willy— down to little Temperance, all, all!'

'That is right, Honor, comb his head with a rake and the locks will lie smooth.'

Both Honor and Charles looked up. Hillary stood before them in the doorway. The girl had turned her face to her brother, and had not observed his approach. She was ill-pleased at his arrival. She wished no stranger to intermeddle with her family troubles.

'You here?' exclaimed Charles, starting to one knee. 'Mr. Larry Nanspian, I owe you something, and I shall repay it when the occasion comes. Not now, though I have a mind to it, because I have a headache. But I can order you off the premises. Get along, or I'll kick you.'

Larry gave a contemptuous shrug with his shoulders, and looked to Honor.

'Well, Honor, have you a good-morning for me?'

'I have ordered you off the premises,' shouted Charles.

'Shall I pitch him into the road again?' asked Larry of the girl.

Then Honor said, 'I did not ask your help yesterday, and I do not seek your interference now.'

Charles burst into a rude laugh. 'You have your answer, Mr. Larry,' he said; 'about face and away with you, and learn that there is one girl in the place whose head you have not turned.'

'If I am not wanted, of course I go,' said Hillary, annoyed.

Then he walked away, whistling, with his hands in his pockets. 'There are more cherries on the tree than that on the topmost twig,' he said to himself in a tone of dissatisfaction. 'If Honor can't be pleasant others are not so particular.'

Larry Nanspian was a spoiled lad. The girls of Bratton made much of him. He was a fine young man, and he was heir to a good estate. The girls not only did not go out of their way to avoid him, but they threw themselves, unblushingly, ostentatiously in his path; and their efforts to catch him were supported by their mothers. The girls hung about the lanes after church hoping to have a word with him, and sighed and cast him languishing glances during Divine worship. Their mothers flattered him. This was enough to make the lad conceited. Only Honor kept away from him. She scarcely looked at him, and held him at a distance. The other girls accepted his most impudent sallies without offence; he did not venture a jest with Honor. Her refusal of the homage which he had come to regard as his due piqued him, and forced him to think of Honor more often than of any other girl in the place. He did not know his own mind about her, whether he liked or whether he disliked her, but he knew that he was chagrined at her indifference.

Sulky, he sauntered on to Broadbury, towards Wellon's Cairn. The moor was stretched around, unbroken by a hedge, or wall, or tree. Before him rose the Tumulus. 'Hah!' he said to himself, 'she was ready to talk to me here; we were to have been good friends, but that cursed White Hare brought us all ill-luck.'

As he spoke to his surprise he saw something white emerge from the cutting in the side. He stood still, and in a moment Mrs. Veale leaped out of the hollow, went over the side, and disappeared down a dyke that ran in the direction of Langford.

The apparition and disappearance were so sudden, the sight of the woman so surprising, that Hillary was hardly sure he was in his senses, and not the prey to a hallucination. He was made very uncomfortable by what he had seen, and instead of going on towards the mound, he turned and walked away.

'This is wonderful,' he said. 'Whatever could take Mrs. Veale to Wellon's Cairn? If it were she—and I'd not take my oath on it—I'm too bewildered to guess her purpose.'

He halted and mused. 'I always said she was a witch, and now I believe it. She's been there after her devilries, to get some bones or dust of the gibbeted man, or a link of his chain, to work some further wickedness with. I'll see Honor again, I will, for all the airs she gives herself, and warn her not to sit on Wellon's mount. It's not safe.'

CHAPTER XII.

LANGFORD.

Honor put on her hat and threw a kerchief over her shoulders, and took her little brother Willy by the hand.

'Whither are you going, Honor?' asked Kate.

'I am going to find a place for Charles, as he will not seek one for himself. I have turned him out of this house, and must secure him shelter elsewhere.'

'Who will have him?' asked Kate contemptuously. She was less forbearing with Charles than Honor. Honor did not answer immediately.

'Try Chimsworthy,' suggested Kate; 'Larry would put in a word for us.'

Honor slightly coloured. She put on her red cloak.

'I cannot, Kate. Larry and Charles have quarrelled.'

'Larry bears no grudges. I will answer for him.'

'I do not wish to ask a favour of the Nanspians.'

'Why not?'

Honor made no reply. She clasped the child's hand tightly and closed her lips. Then, without another word, she left the cottage. Kate shrugged her shoulders.

Honor went slowly up the lane to Broadbury; she did not speak to her little brother her head was slightly bowed, she was deep in thought, and hectic spots of colour tinged her cheeks.

'What! Honor, in your scarlet!' exclaimed Larry. She looked up in surprise. He had come up to Broadbury the second time that day, drawn there irresistibly by desire to see Honor. He thought it probable, as the day was fine, that she would go there with her knitting.

'What has brought you to Broadbury in this array, Honor?' asked Hillary, standing before her, and intercepting her path.

'I am on my road to Langford,' answered the girl with composure.

'Take care, Honor, take care where you go. There is a witch there, Mrs. Veale; if you get in her bad books you will rue it. I have seen her to-day at Wellon's Cairn gathering the dead man's dust, out of which to mix some hell-potion.'

Honor shook her head.

'It is true,' said Hillary earnestly; 'she jumped and ran—and her ways were those of that white hare we saw at the mound. Nothing will now persuade me that she was not that hare. Do not go on, Honor; leave Langford alone. No luck awaits you there.'

'Nonsense, Larry, you cannot have seen Mrs. Veale up here.'

'I tell you that I did. I saw something white hopping and running, and I am sure it was she in the hole scooped by the treasure-seekers.'

'What can she have wanted there?'

'What but the dust of old Wellon? And what good can she do with that? None—she needs it only for some devilry. Do not go near her, Honor; I have come here on purpose to warn you that the woman is dangerous.'

'I must go on,' said Honor. 'It is kind of you, Larry, but I have business which I must do at Langford. I have never harmed Mrs. Veale, and she will not want to hurt me, But now, Larry, let me say that I am sorry if I offended you this morning. I spoke rather rough, because I was afraid of a quarrel and a fight between you and Charles. Do not take it amiss. Now do not stay me, I must go forward.'

'I will let you go on one promise—that you will not cross Mrs. Veale.'
He caught her hand.

'How can I give offence to her? She is nothing to me, nor I to her. You must really make way, Larry.'

He shook his head. 'I don't like it,' he said; but he could not further stay her.

Langford lies under the brow of Broadbury, looking over the tossing sea-like expanse of hill and dale. It lies at a very considerable elevation, nearly a thousand feet above the sea, and to protect it from the weather is covered with slate, as though mail-clad. Few trees stand about it affording shelter. Honor walked through the yard to the door and thrice knocked. Very tardy was the reply. Mrs. Veale opened the door, and stood holding it with one hand, barring the entrance with her body and the other hand. She was in a light cotton dress, from which the colours had been washed. Her face, her eyes, her hair had the same bleached appearance. Her eyelashes were white, overhanging faded eyes, to which they gave a blinking uncertain look.

'What do you want?' asked the housekeeper, looking at her with surprise and with flickering eyes.

'I have come to see Mr. Langford,' answered Honor; 'is your master at home?'

'My *master*, oh yes!' with a sneer, 'my master is at home—my mistress not yet. Oh no! not yet.'

'I want to see him.'

'You do? Come, this is sharp, quick work. You follow one on another as April on March.'

Honor did not understand her. She thought the woman was out of her mind. She made no reply, but looking firmly at her, said, 'I will go into the kitchen and sit down till your master is disengaged. Is he in the house now?'

'You know he is, and you know who is with him.'

Honor drew her brother after her, and entered. She was too proud to give the woman words.

'What do you want? Where are you going?' asked the housekeeper, standing aside to let Honor pass, but casting at her a look so full of malevolence, that Honor turned down her thumb in her palm instinctively to counteract the evil eye. Honor took a kitchen chair and seated herself. 'I will wait here,' she said, 'till Mr. Langford can see me.'

Mrs. Veale stood, still holding the door, looking at her, her white face quivering, her eyes flickering. The child, startled, crept close to his sister, and clung to her.

Mrs. Veale came forward, without removing her eyes from the girl. 'Take care!' she said in a husky voice. 'Take care! you are not here yet.'

Then Honor laughed.

'Not here, Mrs. Veale? What do you mean? I am here.'

Before the housekeeper could speak again men's voices were audible in the passage, and, to her astonishment, Honor recognised that of her father. She rose at once, and confronted him and Taverner Langford as they entered the kitchen.

'What—you here?' exclaimed Oliver Luxmore with undisguised astonishment. 'Why, Honor, what in the world has drawn you to Langford? I did not know that you and Mrs. Veale were friends.'

'I have come to speak to Mr. Langford,' was her reply, spoken quietly; 'but I am glad, father, that you are here, as I should prefer to speak before you. May we go into the parlour?'

She looked at Mrs. Veale, as much as to say that she did not care to speak before witnesses.

'Mrs. Veale,' said Langford, with a sharp tone, 'I heard steps from the parlour door two minutes ago. I object to listeners at key-holes. Do you understand?'

He did not wait for an answer, but turned and led the way down the passage he and Luxmore had just emerged from.

Little Willy uttered a cry. 'Don't leave me with the old woman, please, please, Honor!'

'You shall come with me,' answered the girl, and she drew the child with her into the parlour.

'Here we are,' said Taverner, shutting the door. 'Take a seat, take a seat! The little boy can find a stool at the window.'

'Thank you, Mr. Langford, I will not detain you five minutes. I prefer to stand. I am glad my father is here. Doubtless he has come on the same matter as myself.'

The two men exchanged glances.

'I have come to ask you to try Charles,' she continued. 'Some little while ago you told father that you wanted a man to act as drover for you. I have not heard that you have met with such a servant. Try my brother Charles. He is doing no work now, and Satan sets snares in the way of the idle. If you will please to give him a chance, you will confer on us a great favour, and be doing a good work as well, for which the Lord will reward you.'

'That is what has brought you here?' asked the yeoman.

'Yes, sir.'

'Have you heard it said throughout the country that I am not a man to grant favours?'

'I do not heed what folks say. Besides, I know that this is not so. You have already acted very kindly to us. You lent father a very good horse.'

'Why have you not applied elsewhere? at Chimsworthy, for instance.'

'Because I do not wish to be beholden to the Nanspians, sir,' answered Honor.

'You do not approve of your sister keeping company with that Merry

90

Andrew,' said Taverner approvingly.

'She does not keep company with him,' answered the girl gravely.

At any rate she lets him dance after her, draws him on. Well, well! it is natural, perhaps. But don't advise her to be too eager. Young Larry is not so great a catch as some suppose, and as he and his father give out. Look at Chimsworthy—a wilderness of thistles, and rushes springing where grass grew to my recollection. There is no saying, some day you may be seated at Coombe Park, and then the Nanspians will be below you.'

'Coombe Park!' echoed Honor, looking at her father, then at old Langford. 'Surely, sir, you think nothing of that! Do not encourage father in that fancy; we never were and never will be at Coombe Park.'

'Honor!' exclaimed Oliver Luxmore, working his feet uneasily under the table, 'there you are wrong. The Luxmores have had it for many generations. You have only to look in the registers to see that.'

'Yes, father, some Luxmores have been there, but not our Luxmores as far as we know. I wish you would not trouble your head about Coombe Park. We shall never get it. I doubt if we have a thread of a right to it. If we have, I never saw it.'

'We shall see, we shall see,' said the carrier. 'Girls haven't got lawyers' minds, and don't follow evidence.'

'I have undertaken to go with your father to Lawyer Physick at Okehampton,' said Taverner Langford, 'and to help him to have his right examined.'

'Nothing can come of it but heart-breakings,' sighed Honor; 'father will slip certainties to seize shadows.'

'I have nothing to lose,' said Oliver, 'and much to gain.'

Honor knew it was in vain to attempt to disabuse him of his cherished delusion. She so far shared his views as to believe that the family had gentle blood in their veins, and were descended somehow, in some vague, undefined manner, from the Luxmores of Coombe Park, through, perhaps, some younger son of a junior branch, and she liked to suppose that the beauty and superiority of manner in her brothers and sisters were due to this, but she did not share in her father's expectations of recovering the property. Her understanding was too clear to harbour this.

'I will go back to what I asked of Mr. Langford,' she said, after a pause. 'Will you take my brother Charles into your service, sir? He wants a firm hand over him. He is not bad at heart, but he is infirm of purpose, easily led astray. If he were here with you, he would be far from the "Ring of Bells," and his work would sever him from idle companions.'

'So, you don't want him to be at Chimsworthy?'

'I do not desire to be under obligation there.'

'You have no objection to placing yourself under obligation to me?'

Honor did not like the tone. She did not understand his returning to the same point; she turned uneasily to her father, and asked him to put in a word for poor Charles.

'Mr. Langford is more likely to grant a boon to you than to me,' answered Oliver evasively.

'Sit down, Honor,' he said. 'You have remained standing the whole time you have been here.'

'I have been making a request,' she answered.

'The request is granted. Sit down.'

She was reluctant, yet unwilling to disoblige.

Oliver signed to her to take a place. She obeyed. She was uncomfortable. There was an indefinable something in the way in which the old yeoman looked at and addressed her, something equally indefinable in her father's manner, that combined to disturb her.

Mrs. Veale came in on some excuse, to ask her master a question, with her white eyelashes quivering. She cast a sidelong glance at Honor full of malice, as she entered. When she left the room she did not shut the door, and the girl saw her white face and flickering eyes turned towards her, watching her out of the darkness of the passage. She was for a moment spellbound, but recovered herself when Taverner Longford, with an impatient exclamation, slammed the door.

'I shall be glad to be rid of the old prying cat,' he said.

'Is Mrs. Veale going to leave you?' asked Honor. Then she caught her father and Langford exchange glances, and her brow became hot—she hardly knew wherefore.

'I am thinking of a change,' said the yeoman.

'I hope you are going to have as good a housekeeper,' said Honor; 'a better you cannot have.'

'Oh!' he laughed, 'a better, certainly, and—what is quite as certain—a prettier one. If I had not been sure of that, I would not have——' He checked himself and nodded to the carrier, who laughed.

Honor looked from one to the other inquiringly, then asked somewhat sternly, 'You would not have—what, Mr. Langford?'

'Humph! I would not have taken Charles.'

'What is the connection?' asked the girl.

'More things are connected than sleeve-links,' answered Langford. 'I would not have let your father have the horse if you were thriftless at home. I would not take Charles into service, unless I thought to find in him some of the qualities of the sister.'

'Put my qualities, such as they are, on one side,' said Honor roughly.

'That,' said Langford, looking across at Luxmore, 'that is not to be thought of.'

Then the carrier laughed nervously, and with a side glance at his daughter.

Honor coloured. She was offended, but unable to say at what. She put her hand on her little brother's head and stroked it nervously.

Then the yeoman began to talk to the carrier about his estate, the quality of the land, his cows and horses, his woods, his pastures, the money he was able to put away every year, and contrasted his style of farming with that of the Nanspians at Chimsworthy. As he spoke he fixed his eyes on Honor, to see if his wealth impressed her. But her face expressed no concern. It was clouded; she was thinking, not listening.

All at once the insinuations of Mrs. Veale rushed into her mind. She saw her meaning. She connected that with the looks of the two men. Blood rushed to her face. She sprang to her feet. The room swam before her eyes.

'I must go,' she said. 'I am wanted at home.'

CHAPTER XIII.

THE REVEL.

If to Sally in our alley and the apprentice who loved her, 'Of all the days within the week there was no day but one day,' so to all the maids and all the lads in country villages, in olden times, there was no day in all the year that might compare with the day of the village Revel.

The Revel is now a thing of the past, or lingers on, a limp and faded semblance of the robust festival that fifty years ago was looked forward to through half the year, and looked back on through the other half, and formed the topic of conversation for the entire twelve months.

On Revel day horse-races were run, got up by the village taverner, for a plated mug or a punch ladle; wrestling matches were played for a champion belt, booths were set up in streets of canvas and board for the sale of brooches, ribbons, toys, sweetstuff, and saffron-cakes. There were merry-go-rounds, peep-shows, menageries, and waxworks. The cheap-jack was never wanting, the focus of merriment.

In and about 1849 the commons were enclosed on which the races had been run, and the tents pitched, and gipsies had encamped. Magistrates, squires, parsons, and police conspired against Revels, routed them out of the field, and supplied their places with other attractions,—cottage-garden shows, harvest thanksgivings, and school teas.

Possibly there were objectionable features in those old Revels which made their abolition advisable, but the writer remembers none of these. He saw them through the eyes of a child, and recalls the childish delight they afforded.

The day was clear and sunny. People streamed into Bratton Clovelly from the country round, many on foot, others in gigs and carts, all in gayest apparel. Honor had dressed the children neatly, had assumed her scarlet cloak, and stood at the cottage door turning the key ready to depart with the little eager company, when the tramp of a horse's hoof was heard, and Larry Nanspian drew up before the house. He was driving his dappled cob in the shafts of a two-wheeled tax-cart.

'What, Larry!' exclaimed Kate, 'mounted on high to display the flowery waistcoat? Lost your legs that you cannot walk a mile?'

'Not a bit, sharp-tongue,' answered the young man, good-naturedly. 'I have come round for Honor and you and the little ones.'

'We have feet, sixteen among us.'

'But the tiny feet will be tired with trotting all day. You will have fairings moreover to bring home.'

'Thank you for the kind thought, Larry,' said Honor, softened by his consideration and by the pleasant smile that attended his words. 'Kate and I will walk, but we accept your offer for the children.'

'I cannot take them without you,' said the young man. 'I hold the whip with one hand and the reins with the other. I have not a third wherewith to control a load of wriggling worms.'

'Jump in, Honor,' said Kate; 'sit between me and the driver, to keep the peace.'

The eldest sister packed the children in behind and before, then, without more ado, ascended the seat by Larry, and was followed by Kate, with elastic spring.

'Heigho!' exclaimed the young man, 'I reckon no showman at the Revel has half so fine wares as myself to exhibit.'

'What, the waistcoat?' asked Kate, leaning forward to look in his face.

'No, not the waistcoat,' answered he; 'cutlery, keen and bright.'

'Your wit must have gone through much sharpening.'

'I do not allude to my wit. I mean the pretty wares beside me.'

'But, driver, the wares are not and never will be yours.'

As they drew near Bratton they heard a shout from behind, and turning saw Taverner Langford driving in, with Mrs. Veale beside him, at a rattling pace. Larry drew aside to let them pass; as they went by Taverner looked keenly at Honor, and Mrs. Veale cast her a spiteful glance, then turned to her master and whispered something.

'Upon my word!' exclaimed Larry, 'I've a mind to play a lark. Say nothing, girls, but don't be surprised if we give Uncle Langford a hare-hunt.'

He drew rein and went slow through the street of the 'church town.' The street and the open space before the church gate were full of people. It was, moreover, enlivened with booths. Larry was well content to appear in state at the fair, driving instead of walking like a common labourer, and driving with two such pretty girls as Honor and Kate at his side. He contrasted his company to that of his uncle. 'I wonder my uncle don't get rid of that Mrs. Veale. No wonder he has turned sour with her face always before him.' He shouted to those who stood in the road to clear the way; he cracked his whip, and when some paid no attention brought the lash across their shoulders. Then they started aside, whether angry or good-humoured mattered nothing to the thoughtless lad.

He drew up before the 'Ring of Bells,' cast the reins to the ostler, jumped out, and helped the sisters to descend, then lifted the children down with a cheerful word to each.

The little party strolled through the fair. Honor holding Charity by her left and Temperance by her right hand; but the crowd was too great for the youngest to see anything. Honor stooped and took the little girl on her right arm, but immediately Larry lifted the child from her to his shoulder.

'See!' whispered Joe, holding a coin under Kate's eyes, 'Larry Nanspian gived me this.'

'And I have something; too from him,' said Pattie.

'And so have I,' whispered Willy.

Honor pretended not to hear, but she was touched, and looked with kindly eyes at the young man. He had his faults, his foolish vanity; but there was good in him, or he would not trouble himself about the little ones. She had not been able to give the children more than a penny each for fairing. The village was thronged. The noise was great. The cheap-jack shouted in a voice made hoarse by professional exercise. The ringers had got to the bells in the church tower. At a stall was a man with a gun, a target, and a tray of nuts, calling 'Only a halfpenny a shot!' There was Charles there trying the gun, and his failures to hit the bull's-eye elicited shouts of laughter, which became more boisterous as he lost his temper. The barrel was purposely bent to prevent a level shot reaching the mark. A boy paraded gaudy paper-mills on sticks that whirled in the wind—only one penny each. A barrel organ ground forth, 'The flaxen-headed Plowboy,' and a miserable blinking monkey on it held out a tin for coppers. Honor was so fully engrossed in the children, watching that they did not stray, get knocked over or crushed, that she had not attention to give to the sights of the fair; but Kate was all excitement and delight. Larry kept near the sisters, but could not say much to them: the noise was deafening and little Temperance exacting.

Presently the party drew up before a table behind which stood a man selling rat poison. A stick was attached to the table, and to this stick was affixed a board, above the heads of the people, on which was a pictorial representation of rats and mice expiring in attitudes of mortal agony. The man vended also small hones. He took a knife, drew the edge of the blade over his thumb to show that it was blunt, then swept it once, twice, thrice, this way, that way, on the bit of stone, and see! he plucked a hair from his beard, and cut, and the blade severed it. Fourpence for a small stone, six-pence, a shilling, according to sizes. The coins were tossed on the table, and the hones carried away.

'What is it, ma'am.—a hone?' asked the dealer.

'No, the poison.'

A white arm was thrust between those who lined the table. Hillary turned, and saw Mrs. Veale.

'Keep it locked up, ma'am. There's enough in that packet to poison a regiment.'

Whether a regiment of soldiers or of rats he did not explain.

At the crockery stall Larry halted, and passed Temperance over to Honor. Now his reason for driving in the spring-cart became apparent. He had been commissioned to purchase a supply of pots, and mugs, and dishes, and plates, for home use. Honor also made purchases at this stall, and the young man carried them for her to his cart, as well as his own supply. Then she lingered at a drapery stall, and bought some strong material for frocks for the youngest sisters. Whilst she was thus engaged, Larry went to a stall of sweetstuff, presided over by a man in white apron, with copper scales, and bought some twisted red and white barbers' poles of peppermint. Immediately the atmosphere about the little party was impregnated with the fragrance of peppermint.

A few steps beyond was a menagerie. A painted canvas before the enclosure of vans represented Noah's ark, with the animals ascending a plank and entering it by a door in the side. In another compartment was a picture of a boa-constrictor catching a negro, and opening his jaws to swallow him. Over this picture was inscribed, 'Twine, gentle evergreen,' and the serpent was painted emerald. In another compartment, again, was a polar scene, with icebergs and white bears, seals and whales.

'Oh, we must see the wild beasts!' exclaimed Kate.

A consultation ensued. Larry wished to treat the whole party, but to this Honor would not agree. Finally, it was decided that Kate, Joe, and Pattie should enter, and that Honor should remain without with the children. Accordingly the three went in with Larry, and presently returned disappointed and laughing. The menagerie had resolved itself into a few moulting parrots, a torpid snake in a blanket, two unsavoury monkeys, and an ass painted with stripes to pass as a zebra.

Adjoining the menagerie was another exhibition, even more pretentious. Three men appeared before it on a platform, one with a trumpet, another with cymbals, the third with a drum. Then forth leaped clown, harlequin and columbine, and danced, cut jokes, and went head over heels. The clown balanced a knife on his nose; then bang! toot, toot! clash! bang, bang, bang! from the three instruments, working the children into the wildest speculation. Honor had spent the money laid aside for amusement, and could not afford to take her party in, and she would accept no further favours from Larry.

Just then up came Charles.

'Halloo, mates! you all here!' he shouted, elbowing his way to them. 'That is prime. I will treat you; I've a yellow boy,' he spun a half-sovereign in the air and caught it between both palms. 'Come along, kids. I'm going to treat half a dozen young chaps as well. Shall I stand for you, Larry?' he asked contemptuously, 'or have the thistles and rushes sold so well you can afford to treat yourself?'

Larry frowned. 'I see my father yonder signing to me,' he said. 'I must go to him.'

Then Hillary worked his way to the rear, offended at the insolence of Charles, red in face, and vowing he would not do another kindness to the family.

Old Nanspian was in the long-room of the 'King of Bells,' at the window. He had caught sight of his son, whose flowered satin waistcoat was conspicuous, and was beckoning to him with his clay pipe; he wanted to know whether he had bought the crockery—*vulgo* 'cloam'—as desired, and what he had paid for it.

'Come on, you fellows!' called Charles to some of his companions. 'How many are you? Six, and myself, and the two girls, that makes nine sixpences, and the little tins at half-price makes five threepences. Temperance is a baby and don't count. That is all, five-and-nine; shovel out the change, old girl, four-and-three.'

He threw down the gold coin on the table, where a gorgeous woman in red and blue and spangles, wearing a gilt foil crown and huge earrings, was taking money and giving greasy admission tickets. The circus was small. The seats were one row deep, deal planks laid on trestles. Only at one end were reserved places covered with red baize for the nobility, gentry, and clergy, who, as a bill informed the public, greedily patronised the show. On this occasion these benches were conspicuously empty. The performers appeared in faded fleshings, very soiled at the elbows and knees; the paint on the faces was laid on coarsely; the sawdust in the ring was damp and smelt sour.

The clown cut his jests with the conductor, carried off his cap, and received a crack of the whip. He leaped high in the air, turned a somersault, and ran round the arena on hands and feet, peering between his legs.

A dappled horse was led out, and the columbine mounted and galloped round the ring. Every now and then the hoofs struck the enclosing boards, and the children shrank against Honor and Kate in terror. Then a spray of sawdust was showered over the lads, who roared with laughter, thinking it a joke.

A second horse was led out to be ridden by the harlequin, but the clown insisted on mounting it, and was kicked off. Then the harlequin ran across the area, whilst the horse was in full career, and leaped upon its back, held the columbine's hand, and round and round they went together. All was wretchedly poor. The jokes of the clown were as threadbare as the silks, and as dull as the spangles on the equestrians. Poverty and squalor peered through the tawdry show. But an audience of country folk is uncritical and easily pleased. The jests were relished, the costumes admired, and the somersaults applauded. All at once a commotion ensued. The queen in red and blue, who had sold the tickets of admission, appeared in a state of loud and hot excitement, calling for the manager and gesticulating vehemently. The performance was interrupted. The horses of harlequin and columbine were restrained, and were walked leisurely round the arena, whilst the lady in gauze (very crumpled) seated herself on the flat saddle and looked at the spectators, who curiously scrutinised her features and compared opinions as to her beauty. Presently the clown ran to the scene of commotion. The queen was in very unregal excitement, shaking her head, with her pendant earrings flapping, very loud and vulgar in voice; some of the audience crowded about the speakers.

Then Honor was aware that faces and fingers were pointed towards the bench which she and her party occupied, and in another moment the manager, the crowned lady-manageress, the clown, now joined by the harlequin, who had given his horse to a boy, and a throng of inquisitive spectators, came down—some across the arena, others stumbling over the deal benches—towards the little party.

'That's he!' shouted the lady in crimson and blue, shaking her black curls, puffing with anger, and indicating with a fat and dirty hand, 'That's the blackguard who has cheated us.' She pointed at Charles.

The columbine drew rein and stood her horse before the group, looking down on it. She had holes in her stockings, and the cherry silk of her bodice was frayed. Kate saw that.

'Look here, you rascal! What do you mean by trying to cheat us poor artists, with horses and babies to feed, and all our wardrobe to keep in trim, eh? What do you mean by it?'

Then the clown in broad cockney, 'What do you mean by it, eh? Some one run for the constable, will you? Though we be travelling showmen we're true-born Britons, and the law is made to protect all alike.'

'What is the matter?' asked Honor, rising, with the frightened Temperance in her arms clinging to her neck and screaming, and Charity and Martha holding her skirts, wrapping themselves in her red cloak and sobbing.

'Ah, you may well ask what is the matter!' exclaimed the queen. 'If that young chap belongs to you in any way, more's the pity.'

'It is an indictable offence,' put in the manager. 'It is cheating honest folk; that is what it is.'

Charles burst out laughing.

'I've a right to pay you in your own coin, eh?' he said contemptuously, thrusting his hands into his pockets, and planting a foot on the barrier.

'What do you mean by our own coin?' asked the angry manageress, planting her arms akimbo.

'Giving false for false,' mocked Charles.

'It is insulting of us he is!' exclaimed the columbine, from her vantage post. 'And he calls himself a gentleman.'

'Pray what right have you to invite the public to such a spectacle as this?' asked Charles. 'You have only a couple of screws for horses, and an old girl of forty for columbine, a harlequin with the lumbago, and a clown without wit—and you don't call this cheating?'

'Turn him out!' cried the lady in crumpled muslin, 'it's but twenty-three I am.'

'What is this all about?' asked Honor, vainly endeavouring to gather the cause of the quarrel and compose the frightened children at the same time. The bystanders, indignant at the disparagement of the performance, hissed. All those on the further side of the arena, losing their awe of the sawdust, came over it, crowding round the gauzy columbine and her horse, asking what the row was about, and getting no answer.

The columbine was obliged to use her whip lightly to keep them off. Boys were picking spangles off the saddle-cloth, and pulling hairs out of the mane of the horse.

'How many was it? Fourteen persons let in?' asked the manager.

'And I gave him back change, four-and-three,' added the manageress.

'You shall have your cursed change,' said Charles. 'Get along with you all. Go on with your wretched performance. Here are four shillings, the boys shall scramble for the pence when I find them.' He held out some silver.

'No, I won't take it. You shall pay for all the tickets,' said the woman. 'You ain't a-going to defraud us nohows if I can help It. Let's see, how many was you? Four-and-three from ten makes five-and-nine.'

'I can't do it,' said Charles, becoming sulky. 'If you were the fool to accept a brass token you must pay for the lesson, and be sharper next time. I have no more money.'

'Cheat! cheat! Passing bad money!' the bystanders groaned, hissed, hooted. Charles waxed angry and blazed red. He cursed those who made such a noise, he swore he would not pay a halfpenny, he had no money. They might search his pockets. They might squeeze him. They would get nothing out of him. They might keep the brass token, and welcome, he had nothing else to give them. He turned his pockets out to show they were empty.

The whole assembly, performers in tights, muslin, velvets, ochre and whitening, the spectators—country lads with their lasses, farmers and their wives—were crushed in a dense mass about the scene of altercation. Many of the lads disliked Charles for his swagger and superiority, and were glad to vent their envy in groans and hisses. The elder men thought it incumbent on them to see that justice was done; they called out that the money must be paid.

Charles, becoming heated, cast his words about, regardless whom he hurt. The manager stared, the queen screamed, the clown swore, and columbine, who held a hoop, tried to throw it over the head of the offender, and pull him down over the barrier. By a sudden movement the young man wrenched the whip from the hand of the manager, and raising it over his head threatened to clear a way with the lash. The people started back. Then into the space Honor advanced.

'What has he done? I am his sister. Show me the piece of money.'

'Look at that—and turn yeller,' exclaimed the manager's wife. 'Darn it now, if I ain't a-gone and broke one o' them pearl drops in my ear. Look at the coin,' she put the token into the girl's hand. 'What do yer say to that?' Then she whisked her head of curls about as if to overtake her ear and see the wreck of pearl-drop—silvered glass which had been crushed in the press. 'And this also, young man, comes of yer wickedness. What am I to do with one pendant? Can't wear it in my nose like an Injun. Now then, young woman in scarlet, what do yer call that?'

Honor turned the coin over in her palm,

'This is a brass tradesman's token,' she said, 'it is not money. We stand in your debt five-and-ninepence. I have nothing by me. You must trust me; you shall be paid.'

'No, no! we won't trust none of you,' said the angry woman. 'We ain't a-going to let you out without the money. Pay or to prison you walk. Someone run for the constable, and I'll give him a ticket gratis for this evening's entertainment.'

Then many voices were raised to deprecate her wrath. 'This is Honor.' 'Trust Honor as you'd trust granite.' 'Honor in name and Honor in truth.' 'Honor never wronged a fly.' 'Red spider is a lucky insect.' 'Why don't the red spider spin money now?'

'Leave her alone, she's good as gold. She can't help if the brother is a rascal.'

But though many voices were raised in her favour, no hands were thrust into pockets to produce the requisite money.

Honor looked about. She was hot, and her brow moist; her lips quivered; a streak of sun was on her scarlet cloak and sent a red reflection over her face.

'We will not be beholden to you, madam,' she said, with as much composure as she could muster. Then she unloosed her cloak from her neck and from the encircling arms of Temperance. 'There,' she said, 'take this; the cloth is good. It is worth more money than what we owe you. Keep it till I come or send to redeem it.'

She put the scarlet cloak into the woman's hands, then turned, gathered the children about her, and looking at those who stood in front, said with dignity, 'I will trouble you to make way. We will interrupt the performance no longer.'

Then, gravely, with set lips and erect head, she went out, drawing her little party after her, Kate following, flushed and crying, and Charles, with a swagger and a laugh and jest to those he passed, behind Kate.

When they came outside, however, Charles slunk away. The six young men whom Charles had treated remained. They had worked their way along the benches to dissociate themselves from the party of the Luxmores, and put on a look as if they had paid for their own seats. 'We needn't go, for sure,' whispered one to another. 'We be paid for now out of Miss Honor's red cloak.'

CHAPTER XIV.

THE LAMB-KILLER.

Honor could not recover herself at once. Her heart beat fast and her breathing was quick. Her hands that clasped the children twitched convulsively. She looked round at Charles before he slipped away, and their eyes met. His expression rapidly changed, his colour went, his eyes fell before those of his sister. He drew his cap over his face, and elbowed his way through the crowd out of sight.

Honor felt keenly what had occurred; she was the sister of a rogue; the honourable name of Luxmore was tarnished. How would her father bear this? This, the family honour, was the one thing on which he prided himself. And what about Charles? Would not he be forced to leave the place she had found for him? Would Taverner Langford keep in his employ a man who cheated?

But Honor took a more serious view of the occurrence than the general public. Popular opinion was not as censorious as her conscience. Those whom Charles had attempted to defraud were strangers—vagrants belonging to no parish, and without the pale, fair game for a sharp man to overreach. If the public virtue had protested loudly in the show, it was not in the interests of fair dealing, but as an opportunity of annoying a braggart.

Honor, wounded and ashamed, shrank from contact with her acquaintances, and with Kate worked her way out of the throng, away from the fair, and home, without seeing more of Larry.

Kate took Charles's misconduct to heart in a different way from Honor; she was angry, disappointed because her pleasure was spoiled, and fretted. But the children, as they trotted homewards, were not weary of talking of the wonders they had seen and the enjoyment they had had.

In the evening Hillary drove up with his spring-cart, and called the girls out to take their fairings from his trap, some crocks, a roll of drapery, and some other small matters. Hillary was cheerful and full of fun. He repeated the jokes of the cheap-jack, and told of the neighbours that had been taken in. He mentioned whom he had met, and what he had seen. He allowed the dappled horse to stand in the road, with the reins on the ground, whilst, with one foot planted on the steps, he lingered chatting with the girls before their door. He was so bright and amusing that Kate forgot her vexation and laughed. Even the grave Honor was unable to forbear a smile. Of the disturbance in the circus caused by Charles he said nothing, and Honor felt grateful for his tact. He remained talking for half an hour. He carried the girls' parcels into the cottage for them, and insisted on a kiss from the tiny ones. It almost seemed as if he were tarrying for something—an opportunity which did not offer; but this did not occur to the girls. They felt his kindness in halting to cheer them. Their father was not yet returned from the fair. They were not likely to see Charles again that day.

'By the way, Honor,' said Larry, 'you have some lambs, have you not?'

'Yes, five.'

'Can you fasten them and the ewes in at night?'

'No—we have no place. But why? They will not take hurt at this time of the year.'

'Don't reckon on that,' said the young man; 'I've heard tell there is a lamb-killer about. Farmer Hegadon lost three, and one went from Swaddledown last night. Have you not heard? Watches must be set. None can tell whose dog has taken to lamb-killing till it is seen in the act.'

'A bad business for us if we lose our lambs,' said Honor. 'We reckon on selling them and the ewes in the fall, to meet our debt to Mr. Langford for the horse.'

'Then forewarned is forearmed. Lock them up.'

'It can't be done, Larry. You can't pocket your watch when you're without a pocket.'

'In that case I hope the lamb-killer will look elsewhere. That is all. Good-night. But before I go mind this. If you have trouble about your lambs, call on me. I'll watch for you now you have not Charles at your command. We're neighbours and must be neighbourly.'

'Thank you heartily, Larry. I will do so.'

Then the lad went away, whistling in his cart, but as he went he turned and waved his hand to the sisters.

The children were tired and put to bed. Kate was weary and soon left. Honor had to sit up for her father, whose van was in request that day to convey people and their purchases from the fair to their distant homes. After Oliver had come in and had his supper, Honor put away the plates, brushed up the crumbs, set the chairs straight, and went to bed. Kate and the children were sound asleep. Honor's brain was excited, and she kept awake. She was unobserved now, and could let her tears flow. She had borne up bravely all day; the relaxation was necessary for her now. Before her family and the world Honor was reserved and restrained. She was forced to assume a coldness that was not natural to her heart. There was not one person in the house who could be relied on. Her father was devoid of moral backbone. He remembered the commissions of his customers, but his memory failed respecting his duties to his children and the obligations of home. Kate had too sharp a tongue and a humour too capricious to exercise authority. She set the children by the ears. As for the little ones, they were too young to be supposed to think. So Honor had to consider for her father and the other seven inmates of the cottage, also of late for Charles—to have a head to think for nine creatures who did not think for themselves. There was not one of the nine who stood firm, who was not shiftless. There are few occupations more trying to the temper than the setting up of nine-pins on a skittle-floor. Honor did not become querulous, as is the manner of most women who have more duties to discharge than their strength allows. She was overtaxed, but she sheltered herself under an assumption of coldness. Some thought her proud, others unfeeling. Kate could not fathom her. Oliver took all she did as a matter of course. He neither spared her nor applauded her. Perhaps no one in the parish was so blind to her excellence as her father. Kate was his favourite daughter.

Honor dried her tears on the pillow. What would the end be? Kate was at her side fast asleep. Honor leaned on her elbow and looked at her sleeping sister. The moon was shining. A muslin blind was drawn across the window, but a patch of light was on the whitewashed wall, and was brilliant enough to irradiate the whole chamber. Kate's light silky hair was ruffled about her head. She lay with one arm out, and the hand under her head; her delicate arm was bare. Honor looked long at her; her lips quivered, she stooped over Kate and kissed her, and her lips quivered no more. 'How pretty she is,' she said to her own heart; 'no wonder he went away whistling "Kathleen Mavourneen."'

All at once Honor started, as though electrified. She heard the sheep in the paddock making an unwonted noise, and recalled what Larry had said. In a moment she was out of bed, and had drawn aside the window-blind. The sheep and lambs were running wildly about. Some leaped at the hedge, trying to scramble up and over; others huddled against the gate leading to the lane. Honor opened the casement and put forth her head. Then she saw a dark shadow sweep across the field, before which the clustered sheep scattered.

Honor slipped on a few garments, descended the stair, opened the kitchen door, and went forth armed with a stick. The lamb-killer was in the paddock, chasing down one of the flock that he had managed to separate from the rest. Honor called, but her voice was unheeded or unheard, owing to the bleating of the frightened sheep. She ran through the dewy grass, but her pace was as nothing to that of the dog. The frightened lamb fled from side to side, and up and down, till its powers were exhausted; and then it stood piteously bleating, paralysed with terror, and the dog was at its throat and had torn it before Honor could reach the spot.

When she approached the dog leaped the hedge and disappeared through a gap in the bushes at the top. The girl went about the field pacifying the sheep, calling them, and counting them. They came about her skirts, pressing one on another, bleating, entreating protection, interfering with her movements. Two of the lambs were gone. One she had seen killed; a second was missing. She searched and found it; it had been overrun and had got jammed between two rails. In its efforts to escape, it had become injured. Its life was spent with exhaustion and fear, but it was not quite dead. It still panted. She disengaged the little creature, and carried it in her arms into the house, followed by the agitated ewes, whom she could hardly drive back from the garden gate.

Honor did not expect the dog to return that night, but she sat up watching for a couple of hours, and then returned to her bedroom, though not to sleep.

Here was a fresh trouble come upon the family. The loss of two lambs, in their state of poverty, was a serious loss, and she could not be sure that this was the end. The dog might return another night and kill more, and that was a crushing loss to poor people.

Next morning, when Kate and the children heard the news, their distress was great. Many tears were shed over the dead lambs. Kate was loud in her indignation against those who let their dogs rove at night. She was sure it was done on purpose, out of malice. It was impossible to suppose that the owner of a lamb-killer was ignorant of the proclivities of his dog. If they could only find out whose dog it was they would make him pay for the mischief.

'I suppose, father, you will sit up to-night and watch for the brute?'

'I—I!' answered the carrier. 'What will that avail? I never shot anything in my life but one sparrow, and that I blew to pieces. I rested my gun-barrel on the shiver (bar) of a gate, and waited till a sparrow came to some crumbs I had scattered. Then I fired, and a splash of blood and some feathers were all that remained of the sparrow. No, I am no shot. The noise close to my ear unnerves me. Besides, I am short-sighted. No; if the dog takes the lambs, let him, I cannot prevent it.'

'But you must sit up, father.'

'What can I do? If I saw the dog I should not know whose 't was. Honor saw it, she can say whose it was.'

'I do not know. It struck me as like Mr. Langford's Rover, but I cannot be sure; the ash-trees were between the moon and the meadow, and flickered.'

'Oh! if it be Rover we are right.'

'How so, father?'

'Langford will pay if his dog has done the damage.'

'He must be made to pay,' said Kate. 'He won't do it if he can scrape out.'

'I cannot be sure it was Rover,' said Honor. 'I saw a dark beast, but the ash flickered in the wind, and the flakes of moonlight ran over the grass like lambs, and the shadows like black dogs. I was not near enough to make sure. Unless we can swear to Rover, we must be content to lose.'

'Mr. Langford will not dispute about a lamb or two,' said Oliver, rubbing his ear.

'Then he will be different in this to what he is in everything else,' said Kate.

'He won't be hard on us,' said her father. Honor was accustomed to see him take his troubles easily, but he was unwontedly, perplexingly indifferent now, and the loss was grave and might be graver.

'I will watch with you to-night, Honor,' said Kate. 'And what is more, I will swear to Rover, if I see the end of his tail. Then we can charge the lambs at a pound a-piece to old Langford.'

'As for that,' said the father, with a side-glance at his eldest daughter, 'Mr. Langford—don't call him old Langford any more, Kate, it's not respectful—Mr. Langford won't press for the horse. It lies with you whether we have him for nothing or have to return him.'

He spoke looking at Honor, but he had addressed Kate just before. The latter did not heed his words. Honor had been crossing the room with a bowl in her hands. She stood still and looked at him. A question as to his meaning rose to her lips, but she did not allow it to pass over them. She saw that a knowing smile lurked at her father's mouth-corners, and that he was rubbing his hands nervously. The subject was not one to be prosecuted in the presence of her brothers and sisters. She considered a moment, then went into the back kitchen with the bowl. She would make her father explain himself when they were together alone.

Dark and shapeless thoughts passed through her mind, like the shadows of the ash foliage in the moonlight. She was full of undefined apprehension of coming trouble. But Honor had no time to give way to her fears. There was no leisure for an explanation. The dead lambs had to be skinned and their meat disposed of.

Honor was busily engaged the whole morning. She was forced to concentrate her mind on her task, but unable to escape the apprehension which clouded her. It did not escape her that her father's manner changed, as soon as the children were despatched to school and Kate had gone forth. He became perceptibly nervous. He was shy of being in the room with Honor, and started when she spoke to him. He pretended to look for means of fastening up the flock for the night, but he went about it listlessly. His playful humour had evaporated; he seemed to expect to be taken to task for his words, and to dread the explanation. His troubled face cleared when he saw Hillary Nanspian appear at the top of the hedge that divided the Chimsworthy property from the carrier's paddock. The young man swung himself up by a bough, and stood on the hedge parting some hazel-bushes.

'What is this I hear? The lamb-killer been to you last night?'

'Yes, Larry, and I am trying to find how we may pen the sheep in out of reach. I've only the linhay, and that is full.'

'Are you going to sit up?'

'No, Larry, I am not a shot, and like a beetle at night.'

'I'll do it. Where are Kate and Honor? I promised them I would do it, and I keep my word. Little Joe tells me Honor thinks the dog was Rover. What a game if I shoot Uncle Taverner's dog! I hope I may have that luck. Expect me. I will bring my gun to-night.'

CHAPTER XV.

A BOLT FROM THE BLUE.

Honor's kitchen work was done. She came to her father after Larry Nanspian had departed, and said, 'Now, father, I want to know your meaning, when you said that it lay with me whether you should keep the horse or not?'

Then she seated herself near the door, with a gown of little Pattie's she was turning.

'It was so to speak rigmarole,' answered Oliver colouring, and pretending to plait a lash for his whip.

She shook her head. 'You did not speak the words without purpose.'

'We lead a hard life,' said Oliver evasively. 'That you can't deny and keep an honest tongue.'

'I do not attempt to deny it,' she said, threading a needle at the light that streamed in through the open door. The carrier looked at her appealingly. Behind her, seen through the door, was a bank of bushes and pink foxgloves, 'flopadocks' is the local name. He looked at the sunlit picture with dreamy eyes.

'I shouldn't wonder,' he said, 'if there was a hundred flowers on that there tallest flopadock.'

'I should not either,' said Honor without looking off her work. Then ensued another pause.

Presently the carrier sighed and said, 'It be main difficult to make both ends meet. The children are growing up. Their appetites increase. Their clothes get more expensive. The carrying business don't prosper as it ought. Kate, I reckon, will have to go into service, we can't keep her at home; but I don't like the notion—she a Luxmore of Coombe Park.'

'We are not Luxmores of Coombe Park, but Luxmores out of it,' said Honor.

'Coombe Park should be ours by right, and it rests with you whether we get our rights.'

'How so? This is the second hint you have given that much depends on me. What have I to do with the recovery of Coombe Park? How does the debt for the horse rest with me?'

'It is a hard matter to be kept out of our rights,' said Oliver. 'A beautiful property, a fine house and a fishpond—only a hundred pounds wanted to search the registers to get it.'

'No hundred pounds will come to us,' said Honor. 'The clouds drop thunderbolts, not nuggets. So as well make up our minds to be where we are.'

'No, I can't do that,' said the carrier, plaiting vigorously. 'You haven't got a bit of green silk, have you, to finish the lash with?'

'Whether from wishing or from working, no hundred pounds will come,' continued the girl.

'And see what a rain of troubles has come on us,' said the carrier. 'First comes your poor mother's death, then the horse, now the lambs, and on top of all poor Charles.'

'More the reason why we should put aside all thought of a hundred pounds.'

'Providence never deserts the deserving,' said Luxmore. 'I'm sure I've done my duty in that state o' life in which I am. It is darkest before dawn.'

'I see no daylight breaking.'

'Larry Nanspian makes great count of Kate,' mused Luxmore, and then abruptly, 'confound it! I've plaited the lash wrong, and must unravel it again.'

'What will come of Larry's liking for Kate? Will that bring us a hundred pounds and Coombe Park?' asked Honor bluntly.

'I can't quite say that. But I reckon it would be a rare thing to have her settled at Chimsworthy.'

'No,' said Honor, 'not unless Larry alters. Chimsworthy grows weeds. The old man is more given to boasting than to work. Larry cares more to be flattered than to mind the plough.'

'I won't have a Luxmore of mine marry out of her station. We must hold up our heads.'

'Of course we must,' said Honor. 'What am I doing all day, thinking of all night, but how we may keep our heads upright?'

'What a mercy it would be not to be always fretting over ha'pence! If you and Kate were well married, what a satisfaction it would be to me and what a comfort all round.'

'Do not reckon on me,' said Honor; 'I shall not marry, I have the children to care for. You do not want to drive me out of the house, do y', father?'

'No, certainly not. But I should like to see you and Kate well married, Kate to Larry Nanspian and Chimsworthy, and you—well, you equally well placed. Then you might combine to help me to my own. Consider this, Honor! If we had Coombe Park, all our troubles would clear like clouds before a setting sun. Charles would no longer be a trouble to us. He shows his gentle blood by dislike for work. If he were not forced to labour he would make a proper gentleman. Why then, Honor, what a satisfaction to you to have been the saving, the making of your brother!'

'*Then* won't stand on the feet of *If*,' said Honor.

'It depends on you.'

'How on me?' she rested her hands on her lap, and looked steadily at her father. He unravelled his lash with nervous hands. Honor saw that they shook. Then without turning his eyes from his plaiting, he said timidly, 'I only thought how well it would be for us if you were at Langford.'

'How can I be at Langford? Mrs. Veale is the housekeeper, and I do not wish for her place.'

'Oh no, not her place—not her place by any means,' said her father.

'What other place then?' she was resolved to force him to speak out, though she guessed his meaning.

He did not answer her immediately. He looked at the 'flopadocks' through the front door, then he looked to see if there was a way of escape open by the back.

'I—I thought—that is to say—I hoped—you might fancy to become Mrs. Langford.'

Honor rose proudly from her seat, and placed her needlework in the chair. She stood in the doorway, with the illumined hedge behind her. If Oliver had looked at her face he could not have seen it; he would have seen only the dark head set on a long and upright neck, with a haze of golden brown about it. But he did not look up; he drew a long breath. The worst was over. He had spoken, and Honor knew all.

In the morning the carrier had flattered himself it would be easy to tell Honor, but when he prepared to come to the point he found it difficult. He knew that the proposal would offend his daughter, that it would not appear to

116

her in the light in which he saw it. He was afraid of her, as an inferior nature fears one that is greater, purer than itself. Now he felt like a schoolboy who has been caught cribbing, and expects the cane.

'You see, Honor,' said he in an apologetic tone, 'Taverner Langford is a rich man, and of very good family. It would be no disgrace to him to marry you, and you cannot reckon to look higher. I don't know but that his family and ours date back to Adam. He has kept his acres, and we have lost ours. However, with your help, I hope we may recover Coombe Park and our proper position. What a fine thing, Honor, to be able to restore a fallen family, and to be the means of saving a brother! Taverner Langford is proud, and would like to see his wife's relations among the landed gentry. He would help us with a hundred pounds. Indeed, he has almost promised the money. As to the horse, we need not concern ourselves about that, and the lambs need trouble you no more. There is a special blessing pronounced on the peace-makers, Honor, and that would be yours if you married Taverner, and Kate took Hillary, for then Langford must make up his quarrel with the Nanspians.'

Honor reseated herself, and put her work back on her lap. Oliver had not the courage to look at her face, or he would have seen that she was with difficulty controlling the strong emotion that nigh choked her. He sat with averted eyes, and maundered on upon the advantages of the connection.

'So,' exclaimed Honor at length, 'Taverner Langford has asked for me to be his wife! But, father, he asked before he knew of that affair yesterday. That alters the look. He will back out when he hears of Charles's conduct.'

'Not at all. I saw him yesterday evening, and he laughed at the story. He took it as a practical joke played on the circus folk—and what harm? Everyone likes his jokes, and the Revel is the time for playing them.'

'He has not dismissed Charles?'

'Certainly not.'

'I would have done so, had he been my servant.'

Then she leaned her head on her hand and gazed before her, full of gloomy thought. Her father watched her, when he saw she was not looking at him.

'The advantage for Charles would be so great,' he said.

'Yes,' she exclaimed, with a tone of impatience. 'But there are some sacrifices it is not fair to expect of a sister.'

'Consider that, instead of being a servant in the house, Charles would regard himself as at home at Langford. He is not a bad fellow, his blood is against his doing menial work. When he mounts to his proper place you will see he will be a credit to us all. You don't take razors to cut cabbages. I, also, will no longer be forced to earn my livelihood by carrying. If your mind be healthy, Honor, you will see how unbecoming it is for a Luxmore to be a common carrier. Lord bless me! When I am at Coombe Park, you at Langford, and Kate at Chimsworthy, what a power we shall be in the place. Why, I may even become a feoffee of Coryndon's Charity! Langford is rich. He has a good estate. He has spent nothing on himself for many years. There must be a lot of money laid by somewhere. He cannot have saved less than three hundred pounds a year, and I should not stare to hear he had put by five. Say this has been going on for twenty years. That amounts to ten thousand pounds at the lowest reckoning. Ten thousand pounds! Think of that, Honor. Then remember that old Hillary Nanspian is in debt to Taverner Langford, and pressed to raise the money, as the debt has been called up. You must persuade Taverner to let the money lie where it is, and so you will bring peace to Chimsworthy.'

Honor shook her head.

'It cannot be, father,' she said, in a low tone.

'I feared you would raise difficulties,' he said, in an altered, disappointed voice. 'Of course he is too old for you. That is what you girls think most about.'

She shook her head.

'Perhaps you have fancied someone else,' he went on; 'well, we can't have plum cake every day. It is true enough that Taverner Langford is not a yellow gosling; but then he has ten thousand pounds, and they say that a young man's slave is an old man's darling. He won't live for ever, and then you know——'

Honor's cheeks flushed; she raised her head, passed her hand over her brow, and looking at her father with dim eyes, said, 'That is not it—no, that is not it.' Then with an access of energy, 'I will tell you the real truth. I cannot marry whom I do not love, and I cannot love whom I do not respect. Mr. Langford is a hard man. He has been hard on his kinsman, Mr. Nanspian, and though the old man had a stroke, Mr. Langford never went near him, never sent to ask how he was, and remained his enemy. About what? I've heard tell about a little red spider. Mr. Langford may be rich, but he loves his money more than his flesh and blood, and such an one I cannot respect.'

The carrier forced a laugh. 'Is not this pot falling foul of kettle?' he asked. 'Who is hard if you are not? Have you shown gentleness to Charles, who is your very brother? Whereas Nanspian is but a brother-in-law.'

'I have not been hard with Charles. I must protect the children from him. He is my brother, and I love him. But I love the others also. I will do all I can for him, but I will not have the others spoiled for his amusement.'

'We don't all see ourselves as others see us,' said Oliver sulkily. Honor was stung by his injustice, but she made no reply. She took up her sewing again, but she could not see to make stitches. She laid her work again on her lap, and mused, looking out of the door at the fox-gloves, and the honeysuckle and wild rose in the hedge. The scent of the honeysuckle was wafted into the room.

'Why should Mr. Langford want me as his wife?' she asked dreamily; 'surely Mrs. Veale will suit him better. She is near his age, and accustomed to his ways. Besides,' she paused, then resumed, 'there have been queer tales about him and her.'

'Pshaw, Honor! a pack of lies.'

'I have no doubt of that,' she said; 'still—I cannot see why he wants me.'

'Honor, my child,' said her father slowly and with his face turned from her; 'he and Nanspian of Chimsworthy don't hit it off together, and the property is so left that if he hasn't children it will pass to his sister's son, young Larry. The old man can't bear to think of that, and on their reckoning on his dead shoes, and he'd draw a trump from his pack against those Nanspians.'

Honor flamed crimson and her eyes flashed. 'And so—so this is it! I am to help to widen the split! I am to stand between Larry and his rights! Father, dear father, how can you urge me? How can you hope this? No, never, never will I consent. Let him look elsewhere. There are plenty of maidens in Bratton less nice than me. No, never, never will I have him.'

Oliver Luxmore stood up, troubled and ashamed.

'You put everything upside down,' he said; 'I thought you would be a peace-maker.'

'You yourself tell me that I am chosen out of spite to make the strife hotter. Now you have told me the why, the matter is made worse. Such an offer is an outrage. Never, father, no, never, never,' she stamped, so strong, so intense was her disgust. 'I will hear no more. I grieve that you have spoken, father. I grieve more that you have thought such a thing possible. I grieve most of all that you have wished it.'

'Turn the offer over in your mind, Honor,' he said sauntering to the door, from which she had withdrawn. She was leaning against the wall between the door and the window, with her hands over her face. 'Milk runs through the fingers when first you dip 'em, but by turning and turning you turn out butter. So, I dare be bound, the whole thing will look different if you turn it over.'

'I will put it away from me, out of my thought,' she said hotly. She was hurt and angry.

'If you refuse him we shall have to buy a horse.'

'Well, we must buy. I will work the flesh from my fingers till I earn it, and get out of obligation. But I never, never, never will consent to be Taverner Langford's wife, not for your sake, father, nor for that of Charles.'

'Well,' said the carrier; 'some folks don't know what is good for 'em. I reckon there's a hundred bells on that there flopadock. I'll go and count 'em.'

CHAPTER XVI.

KEEPING WATCH.

In the evening Hillary the younger arrived, according to promise, with his gun. Oliver Luxmore feebly protested against troubling him. 'It is very good of you, Larry, but I don't think I ought to accept it.'

'It is pleasure, not trouble,' answered Larry.

'If the dog does not come to-night, I will keep guard on the morrow,' said the carrier. 'I may not be able to shoot the dog, but I can scare him away with a bang.'

'I hope to kill him,' said Hillary. 'Have you not heard that a guinea is offered for his carcase? Several farmers have clubbed and offered the reward.'

'Have your lambs suffered, Larry?'

'Ours are all right; driven under cover.'

The young man supped with the Luxmores. He was full of mirth. Kate did not spare her tongue; she attacked and he retaliated, but all good-humouredly. 'They make a pair, do they not?' whispered Oliver to his eldest daughter. 'Better spar before marriage and kiss after, than kiss first and squabble later.'

'Larry,' said Honor, 'I will keep the fire up with a mote (tree-stump). You may be cold during the night, and like to run in and warm yourself.'

'Ay, Honor,' said her father. 'Have a cider posset on the hob to furnish inner comfort.'

'Let no one sit up for me; I shall want nothing,' answered Hillary, 'unless one of you girls will give me an hour of your company to break the back of the watch.'

'Your zeal is oozing out at your elbows,' said Kate. 'Honor or I, or even little Joe, could manage to drive away the dog.'

'But not shoot it,' retorted Hillary. 'Lock your door and leave me without. I shall be content if I earn the guinea.'

'I will remain below,' said Honor quietly. 'We must not let all the burden rest on you. And if you are kind enough, Larry, to look after our lambs, we are bound to look after you.'

'If one of you remains astir, let it be Honor,' said the young man. 'Kate and I would quarrel, and the uproar would keep the dog away.'

'I do not offer to sit up to-night,' said the carrier, 'as my turn comes on the morrow, and I have had heavy work to-day that has tired me.'

Then he rose, held out his hand to Larry, kissed his daughters, and went upstairs to his room. Kate followed him speedily. Larry took up his gun and went out, and walked round the field. Then he came to the kitchen and said, 'All is quiet, not a sign to be seen of the enemy. I hope he will not disappoint me. You must have your red cloak again.'

'My red cloak?' repeated Honor.

'Ay, your red cloak that you parted with to the woman at the circus. I heard about it. If I shoot the dog, half the prize money goes to you.'

'Not so, Larry. It is, or will be, all your own.'

'But you first saw the dog, you share the watch, you keep up the fire, and brew me a posset. How was it with David's soldiers? What was his decision? They that tarried with the stuff should share with those that went to war. You have Scripture against you, Honor, and will have to take ten-and-six.'

'Don't reckon and divide before the dog is shot.'

'If he comes this way he shall sup off lead, never doubt. Then you shall have your red cloak again.'

Honor sighed. 'No, Larry, I shall never see it more. The fair is over, the circus gone, whither I know no more than what has become of yesterday.'

'Charles behaved very badly. Of course I did not mention it before, but we are alone together now, and I may say it.'

'He did not act rightly—he meant it as a joke.'

'I can't forgive him for robbing you of your pretty red cloak. Here, Honor, take it. I have it.'

Then he pulled out a closely folded bundle and extended it to her. The girl was surprised and pleased. This was considerate and kind of Larry. She had noticed him carrying this bundle, but had given no thought as to what it was. Her eyes filled.

'Oh Larry! God bless you for your kindness.'

'I was tempted to hang it round my neck till I gave it back, I should have looked quite military in it.'

'It was my mother's cloak,' she answered quickly. 'You might have worn it and it would have done you good. My mother will bless you out of paradise for your consideration. Oh my dear, dear mother! she was so wise, and thoughtful, and good.' Honor spread the cloak over the young man's head. 'There,' she said, 'take that as if she had touched you. You have lost your mother.'

'Yes, but I do not remember her.'

'Oh! it is a bad thing for you to be without your mother, Larry.' She paused, then held out her hand to him, and her honest eyes met his slowing with gratitude, swimming with feeling.

'All right,' he said. 'No thanks. We are neighbours and good friends. If I help you to-day you will stand by me to-morrow. That is so, is it not, dear Honor?'

He threw his gun over his shoulder and went out into the meadow. He was glad to escape the pressure of her hand; the look of her eyes had made his heart beat with unwonted emotion. She had never given him such a look before. She was not as cold as he supposed. He was aware that he had acted well in the matter of the cloak. He had gone to the manageress of the circus directly he heard what had taken place, and had made an offer for the garment. The woman, seeing his eagerness to secure it, refused to surrender it under a sum more than its value. He had bought it with the sacrifice of the rest of his pocket-money. That was one reason why he hoped to kill the dog. He would replenish his empty purse. In this matter he had acted as his heart dictated, but he was quite aware that he had done a fine thing. Honor paid him his due, and that raised Honor in his estimation. 'She has heart,' he said, 'though she don't often show it. A girl must have heart to do as she did for that worthless brother.'

Whilst Larry stood without waiting for the dog, Honor was within, sitting by the fire, a prey to distressing thoughts. She was not thinking of Larry or of Charles; she was thinking of what had passed between her and her father.

She occupied a low stool on the hearth, rested her head in her lap, folded her hands round her knees. The red glow of the smouldering fire made her head like copper, and gave to her faded red stockings a brilliancy they lacked by day.

She had dimly suspected that something was plotted against her on the occasion of her visit to Langford, when she had found her father with

Langford. What she had dreaded had come to pass. Her father had consented to sell her so as to extricate himself from a petty debt, but, above all, that he might be given means of prosecuting his imaginary claims. Coombe Park was a curse to them. It had blighted Charles, it had spoiled her father's energies, it was doomed to make a breach between her and her father. She had never herself thought of Coombe Park; she had treated its acquisition as an impossible dream, only not to be put aside as absurd because harboured by her father. She was conscious now of a slight stirring of reproach in her heart against him, but she battled it and beat it down. Strong in her sense of filial respect, she would not allow herself to entertain a thought that her father was unjust. She apologised to herself for his conduct. She explained his motives. He had supposed that the prospect of being mistress of a large house, over wide acres, would fill her ambition. He meant well, but men do not understand the cravings of the hearts of women. But, explain away his conduct as she would, she was unable to dissipate the sense of wrong inflicted, to salve the wound caused by his apparent eagerness to get rid of her out of the house. The back door was opened softly.

'Honor! still awake?'

'Yes, Larry.'

'Will you give me a drop of hot cider? I am chilled. Have you a potato sack I can cast over my shoulders? The dew falls heavily.'

'No sign of the dog yet?'

'None at all. The sheep are browsing at ease. It is dull work standing at a gate watching them. I wish the dog would come.'

'Let us change places, Larry. You come by the fire and I will watch at the gate. The moment that I see him I will give warning.'

'And scare him away! No, Honor, I want the prize-money.'

'Then I will come out and keep you company. Here are two potato sacks, one for your shoulders, the other for mine. If we talk in a low tone we shall not warn off the dog.'

'That is well, Honor. So we shall make the hours spin. The moon is shining brightly. There have been clouds, and then the dew did not fall as cold and chill. I have been hearkening to the owls, what a screeching and a hooting they make, and there is one in the apple-tree snoring like my father.'

'Have you been standing all the while, Larry?'

'Yes, Honor, leaning against the gate. If there had been anything to sit on I should have seated myself. My fingers are numb. I must thaw them at your coals.'

He went to the fire and held his hands in the glow. 'Honor!' he said, 'you have been crying. I see the glitter of the tears on your cheeks.'

'Yes, I have been crying—not much.'

'What made you cry?'

'Girl's troubles,' she answered.

'Girl's troubles! What are they?'

'Little matters to those they do not concern. Here is a low stool on which the children sit by the heart. I will take it out and set it under the hedge. We can sit on it and talk together awaiting the dog.'

'What is the time, Honor? Is the clock right? Eleven! I will wait till after midnight and then go. He will not come to-night if he does not come before that. He will have gone hunting elsewhere. Perhaps he remembers that you scared him last night.' Honor carried out a low bench, and placed it near the gate under the hedge where a thorn tree overhung.

'We shall do well here,' said Hillary. 'The dog will not see us, and we shall know he is in the field by the fright of the sheep.'

He seated himself on the bench and Honor did the same, at a distance from him—as far away as the bench permitted. She had thrown the potato sack over her head, and wore it as a hood; it covered her shoulders as well,

126

and shaded her face. The dew was falling heavily, the meadow in the moon was white with it, as though frosted, and through the white sprinkled grass went dark tracks, as furrows, where the sheep had trodden and dispersed the sparkling drops.

'Do you hear the owls?' asked Larry. 'I've heard there are three which are seen every night fleeting over Wellon's Cairn, and that they are the souls of the three women Wellon killed. I've never been there at night, have you, Honor?'

'No, I do not go about at night.'

'I should not like to be on Broadbury after dark, not near the old gibbet hill, anyhow. Listen to the old fellow snoring in the apple-tree. I thought owls slept by day and waked by night, but this fellow is dead asleep, judging by the noise he makes.'

After silence of a few moments, during which they listened to the owls, 'I wonder, Honor,' said the young man, 'that you liked to sit on the mound where Wellon was hung. It's a queer, whisht (uncanny) place.'

'I only sit there by day, and that only now and then when I can get out a bit. I have not been there for some time.'

Then ensued another pause.

'I wish you would tell me one thing,' said the girl, 'yet it is what I have no right to ask. Do you owe Mr. Langford a great deal of money?'

'Oh yes,' answered Hillary carelessly, 'a great deal. He has called it in, and we shall have to pay in a month or two.'

'Can you do so out of your savings?'

'We have no savings. We shall go to Mr. Physick—father and I—and get a mortgage made on the property. It is easily done. I am of age. Father couldn't have done it by himself, but I can join and let him.' He held up his head. He was proud of the consequence gained by consenting to a mortgage.

'The first thing you have to do with the property is to burden it,' said Honor.

Hillary screwed up his mouth.

'You may put it so if you like.' Instead of looking round at him admiring his consequence, she reproached him.

'That is something to be ashamed of, I think,' she said.

'Not at all. If I did not, Uncle Taverner could come down on us and have a sale of our cattle and waggons and what not. But, maybe, that would suit your ideas better?'

'No,' said Honor gravely, 'not at all. No doubt you are right; but you are old enough not to have let it come to this. Your service on the farm ought to have been worth fifty pounds a year for the last four years. I doubt if it has been worth as many shillings.'

He clicked his tongue in the side of his mouth, and threw out his right leg impatiently.

'Mr. Langford has saved thousands of pounds. He puts by several hundreds every year, and his land is no better than yours.'

'Uncle Taverner is a screw.' Then, jauntily, 'we Nanspians are open-handed, we can't screw.'

'But you can save, Larry.'

'If Uncle Taverner puts away hundreds, I wonder where he puts them away?'

'That, of course, I cannot say.'

'I wonder if Mrs. Veale knows?' Then he chuckled, and said, 'Honor, some of the chaps be talking of giving him a hare-hunt. We think he ought to be shamed out of letting that woman tongue-lash him as she does?'

'Larry!' exclaimed Honor, turning sharply on him and clutching his arm, 'for God's sake do not be mixed up in such an affair. He is your uncle, and you may be very unjust.' He shrugged his shoulders.

'I'm not over sweet on Uncle Taverner,' he said. 'It is mean of him calling in that money, and he deserves to be touched up on the raw.'

'Larry, you warned me against Mrs. Veale. Now I warn you to have no hand in this save to hold it back. It must not be; and for you to share in it will be scandalous.'

'How the owls are hooting! To-whoo! Whoo! Whoo! I wonder what sort of voice the old white owl has. He goes about noiseless, like a bit of cotton grass blown by the wind.'

Then Honor went back to what she was speaking of before. 'It goes to my heart to see good land neglected. Your nettle-seeds sow our land, and thistle-heads blow over our hedge. Now that your father is not what he was, you should grasp the plough-handle firmly. Larry, you know the knack of the plough. Throw your weight on the handles. If you do not, what happens?'

'The plough throws you.'

'Yes, flings you up and falls over. It is so with the farm. Throw your whole weight on it, through your arms, or it will throw you.'

'That old snorer is waking,' said Hillary.

'You love pleasure, and do not care for work,' pursued Honor. 'You are good-natured, and are everyone's friend and your own enemy. You shut your eyes to your proper interest and open your purse to the parish. The bee and the wasp both build combs, both fly over the same flowers and enjoy the same summer, but one gathers honey and the other emptiness. Larry, do not be offended with me if I speak the truth. The girls flirt with you and flatter you, and the elder folk call you a Merry Andrew, and say you have no mischief in you, and it is a pity you have not brains. That is not true. You have brains, but you do not use them. Larry, you have no sister and no mother to speak openly to you. Let me speak to you as if I were your sister, and take it well, as it is meant.'

So she talked to him. Her voice was soft and low, her tone tremulous. She was afraid to hurt him, and yet desirous to let him know his duty.

She was stirred to the depth of her heart by the events of the day.

Larry was unaccustomed to rebuke. He knew that she spoke the truth, but it wounded his vanity, as well as flattered it, to be taken to task by her. It wounded him, because it showed him he was no hero in her eyes; it flattered him, because he saw that she took a strong interest in his welfare. He tried to vindicate himself. She listened patiently; his excuses were lame. She beat them aside with a few direct words. 'Do not be offended with me,' she pleaded, turning her face to him, and then the moonlight fell over her noble features; the potato sack had slipped back. 'I think of you, dear Larry, as a brother, as a kind brother who has done many a good turn to us, and I feel for you as an elder sister.'

'But, Honor, you are younger than I am by eighteen months.'

'I am older in experience, Larry; in that I am very, very old. You are not angry with me?'

'No, Honor, but I am not as bad as you make out.'

'Bad! Oh Larry, I never, never thought, I never said you were bad. Far otherwise. I know that your heart is rich and deep and good. It is like the soil of your best meadows. But then, Larry, the best soil will grow the strongest weeds. Sometimes when I look through the gates of Chimsworthy I long to be within, with a hook reaping down and rooting up. And now I am peering through the gates of your honest eyes, and the same longing comes over me.'

He could see by the earnest expression of her face, by the twinkle of tears on her lashes, that she spoke out of the fulness of her heart. She was not praising him, she was rebuking him, yet he was not angry. He looked intently at her pure, beautiful face. She could not bear his gaze, he saw her weakness. He put his finger to her eyelashes. 'The dew is falling heavily, and has dropped some diamonds here,' he said.

She stood up.

'Hark!' she said, and turned her head. 'The cuckoo clock in the kitchen is calling midnight. We need remain here no longer.'

'I should like to remain till day,' said Larry.

'What, to be scolded?'

'To be told the truth, dear Honor.'

'Do not forget what I have said. I spoke because I care for you. The sheep will not be disturbed to-night. Will you have some posset and go home?'

'Your father will keep guard to-morrow night, but the night after that I will be here again. Oh Honor, you will sit up with me, will you not?' He took her hand. 'How much better I had been, how the Chimsworthy coomb would have flowed with honey, had God given me such a sister as you.'

'Well, begin to weed yourself and Chimsworthy,' she said with a smile.

'Will you not give me a word of praise as well as of blame?'

'When you deserve it.'

She pressed his hand, then withdrew it, entered the cottage, and fastened, the door.

Hillary walked away with his gun over his shoulder, musing as he had not mused before.

CHAPTER XVII.

MRS. VEALE.

Charles Luxmore had left the Revel shortly after the departure of his sisters. He returned to Langford covered with shame and full of anger. He was not ashamed of his rascality. He thought himself justified in playing a trick on tricksters. But he was ashamed at being conquered by his sister, and he was unable to disguise to himself that he cut an ignoble figure beside her. At the circus there had been a general recognition of her worth, and as general a disparagement of himself. Why had she interfered? He had courted a 'row' in which he might have held his own against the equestrians, sure of support from the young Brattonians. That would have been sport, better than tumbling in the sawdust and skipping through hoops. If he could only have excited a fight, the occasion would have been forgotten in the results; he would have come out in flaming colours as a gallant fellow. Now, because Honor had interfered and put him in the wrong, he had been dismissed as a rogue.

He knew well enough the red cloak Honor had given away. He knew that it had belonged to her mother, and that Honor prized it highly, and that it was very necessary to her.

Let him excuse himself as he would, a sense of degradation oppressed him which he was unable to shake off.

The behaviour of his comrades had changed towards him, and this galled him. After leaving the circus he had essayed swagger, but it had not availed. His companions withdrew from him as if ashamed to be seen in his society. The popular feeling was roused in behalf of Honor, who was universally esteemed, rather than offended at the fraud played on the equestrians. It was well known that he, Charles, had not behaved towards her with consideration, that he had increased the burden she bore so bravely. This last act was the climax of his wrong-doing. Charles's inordinate vanity had been hurt, and he was angry with everyone but himself.

He returned to the farmhouse, where he had been taken in, cursing the stupidity of the villagers, the meddlesomeness of his sisters, the cowardice of his companions, and his own generosity.

He was without money now, and with no prospect of getting any till his wage was paid.

He turned out his pockets; there was nothing in them, not even the brass token. He too proud to borrow of his boon companions; he questioned whether, if he asked, they would lend him any. He doubted if the innkeeper would let him drink upon trust. How intolerable for him to be without money! To have to lounge his evenings away in the settle before the fire at Langford, or loafing about the lanes! 'I know well enough,' he muttered, 'why the louts keep away from me. 'Tis because they know I'm cleaned out. It's not along of that cursed token, not a bit. If I'd my pockets full they'd be round me again as thick as flies on a cow's nose.'

He had only been a few days in the service of Taverner Langford. He had entered the service rather surlily, only because forced to do so, as Honor refused to allow him to sleep and have meals at home. 'It'll keep me in meat for a bit, and I'll look about me,' he said; 'but it is not the sort o' place for a gentleman—a Luxmore.'

He had not asked leave to take a holiday on the occasion of the Revel. He had taken it as a matter of course. The Revel was a holiday, of course; so is Sunday. 'I don't ask old Langford whether I'm to keep the Sabbath by doing nothing: I do nothing. I don't ask him if I'm to enjoy myself Revel day: I enjoy myself. These are understood things.' He curled his lip contemptuously. 'What a shabby wage I get, or am to get!' he muttered. 'No pay, no work; short pay, short work. That stands to reason—like buttering parsnips.'

He sauntered into the Langford kitchen and threw himself into the settle, with his hat on, and his legs outstretched, and his hands in his pockets. Disappointment, humiliation, impecuniosity combined to chafe his temper, and give him a dejected, hang-dog appearance.

Mrs. Veale passed and repassed without speaking. She observed him without allowing him to perceive that she observed him. Indeed, he hardly noticed her, and he was startled by her voice when she said, as he bent over the fire, 'Charles Luxmore, what do y' think of the Revel now? I've a-been there, and to my reckoning it were grand, but, Lord! you've been over the world, and seen so many fine things that our poor Revel is nought in your eyes, I reckon.'

'Bah! poor stuff, indeed. You should see Bombay, or the bazaar at Candahar! Bratton Clovelly! Bah! Punjab, Cawbul, Delhi, Peshawur! Ghuznee! Hyderabad!' The utterance of these names, which he knew would convey no idea whatever to the mind of Mrs. Veale, afforded him relief. It morally elevated him. It showed him that he knew more of the world than Mrs. Veale. 'You don't happen to know Dost Mahommed?'

'Oh, dear, no!'

'Nor ever heard tell of him?'

'No, Mr. Luxmore.'

'He's an Ameer.'

'Is he now?'

'I've fought him. Leastways his son, Akbar Khan.'

'You wasn't hard on him, I hope?'

'No, I wasn't that. I merely carried off the doors of his mosque.'

'Did that hurt him much?'

'His feelings, Mrs. Veale, awful.'

'Lord bless me!' exclaimed the woman, looking at him over her shoulder as she stirred a pot on the fire, with her queer blinking eyes studying his expression but expressing nothing themselves.

'I do wonder you be home from the Revel so early. A soldier like you, and a fine young chap, ought to have stayed and enjoyed yourself. The best of the fun, I've heard tell, is in the evening.'

'How can I stay at the Revel when I haven't a copper to spend there?' asked Charles surlily.

'I don't like to see a grand young fellow like you sitting at home, like an old man with the rheumatics. We will be friends, Charles. I will give you a crown to buy your good-will.' She took the money from her pocket and handed it him.

'I thank you,' he said grandly—she had called him a grand young man —'but I can't go to the Revel now.' Nevertheless he pocketed the crown. 'I've seen enough of it, and got sick of it. Wretched stalls where nothing is for sale worth buying, wretched shows where nothing is seen worth seeing. I came away because the Revel wearied me.'

'You'll find it dull here,' said the housekeeper. 'We poor ignorant creatures think the Revel and all in it mighty fine things, because we know no better and haven't seen the world. It seems to me, Mr. Luxmore, you're in the wrong place, as the elephant said to the stickleback that had got into the ark.'

'I should just about think I was,' said Charles, kicking out with both his heels. Mrs. Veale was a plain, not to say unpleasant-looking woman, much older than himself; he would not have given her a thought had she not called him 'Mr. Luxmore,' and so recognised that he was a superior being to the Dicks and Toms on the farm.

'Peshawur! Jelalabad! Cawbul! that's how they come,' said Charles. Mrs. Veale stood with hand on the handle of the pan, an iron spoon uplifted in the other, waiting to drink in further information. 'Through the Khyber Pass,' he added, drawing his brows together and screwing up his mouth.

'No doubt about it,' said Mrs. Veale. 'It must be so, if you sez it. And Solomon in all his glory was not arrayed like one of these.' She stirred the pot; then, thinking she had not made herself intelligible, she explained, 'I mean that Solomon, though the wisest of men, didn't know that, I reckon.'

'How could he,' asked Charles, 'never having been there?'

'I do wonder, now, if you'll excuse the remark,' said the housekeeper, 'that you didn't bring the silver belt here and hang it up over the mantel-shelf.'

'Silver belt? What silver belt?'

'Oh! you know. The champion wrestler's belt that is to be tried for this afternoon. I suppose you didn't go in for it because you thought it wouldn't be fair on the young chaps here to take from them everything.'

'I did not consider it worth my while trying for it,' said Charles, with a kick at the hearth with his toes—not an irritated kick, but a flattered, self-satisfied, pleased kick. 'Of course I could have had it if I had tried.'

'Of course you might, you who've been a soldier in the wars, and fought them blood-thirsty Afghans, Lord! I reckon they was like Goliaths of Gath, the weight of whose spear was as a weaver's beam.'

Charles jerked his head knowingly.

'Afghanistan was a hard nut to crack.'

'Ah!' acquiesced Mrs. Veale. 'So said old Goodie as she mumbled pebbles.' Then she stood up and looked at him. 'I know a fine man when I see him,' she said, 'able to hold himself like the best gentleman, and walking with his head in the air as if the country belonged to him.'

'Ah!' said Charles, taking off his hat and sitting erect, 'if all men had their rights Coombe Park would be ours.'

'Don't I know that?' asked the housekeeper. 'Everyone knows that. Nobody can look at you without seeing you're a gentleman born. And I say it is a shame and a sin that you should be kicked out of your proper nest, and it the habitation of strangers, cuckoos who never built it, but have turned out the rightful owners. I reckon it made me turn scarlet as your sister's cloak to see her come crawling here t'other day on bended knees to ask the master to take you in. She's no lady, not got a drop of blue blood in her veins, or she'd not ha' done that. I'll tell you what it is, Mr. Charles. All the gentle blood has run one way and all the vulgar blood the other, as in our barton field the sweet water comes out at the well, and the riddam (ferruginous red water) at the alders.' She spoke with such acrimony, and with a look so spiteful, that Charles asked, 'What has Honor done to offend you?'

'Oh nothing, nothing at all! I don't stoop to take offence at her.' Then, observing that the young man resented this disparagement of his sister, she added hastily, 'There, enough of her. She's good enough to wash and comb the little uns and patch their clothes. We will talk about yourself, as the fox said to the goose, when she axed him if duck weren't more tasty. Why have you come from the Revel? There be some better reason than an empty pocket.'

'I have been insulted.'

'Of course you have,' said Mrs. Veale, 'and I know the reason. The young men here can't abide you. For why? Because you're too much of a gentleman, you're too high for 'em. As the churchyard cross said to the cross on the spire, "Us can't talk wi'out shouting." Do you know what the poacher as was convicted said to the justice o' peace? "I'm not in a position, your worship, to punch your head, but I can spit on your shadow."'

'Without any boasting, I may admit that I and these young clodhopping louts ain't of the same sort,' said Charles proudly.

'That's just what the urchin (hedgehog) said to the little rabbits when he curled up in their nest.'

'Ah!' laughed Charles, 'but the urchin had quills and could turn the rabbits out, and I have not.'

'You've been in the army, and that gives a man bearing, and you've been half over the world, and that gives knowledge; and nature have favoured you with good looks. The lads are jealous of you.'

'They do not appreciate me, certainly,' said Charles, swelling with self-importance.

'This is a wicked world,' said Mrs. Veale. Then she produced a bottle of gin and a glass, and put them at Charles's elbow. 'Take a drop of comfort,' she said persuasively, 'though for such as you it should be old crusted port and not the Plymouth liquor, as folks say is distilled from turnips.'

Young Luxmore needed no pressing; he helped himself.

'I reckon,' pursued Mrs. Veale, 'you were done out of Coombe Park by those who didn't scruple to swear it away. Money and law together will turn the best rights topsy-turvy.'

'No doubt about that, ma'am,' said Charles. 'I've heard my father say, many a time, that with a hundred pounds he could win Coombe Park back.'

'Then why do you not lay out the hundred pounds?'

'Because I haven't got 'em,' answered Charles.

'Oh! they're to be got,' said the housekeeper, 'as the gipsy said to his wife when she told 'n she were partial to chickens.'

'It seems to me,' said the young man, 'that it is a hard world for them that is straight. The crooked ones have the best of it.'

'Not at all,' answered the housekeeper. 'The crooked ones can't go through a straight hole. It is they who can bend about like the ferret as gets on best, straight or crooked as suits the occasion.'

Charles stood up, drank off his glass, and paced the room. The housekeeper filled his glass again. The young man observed her actions and returned to his seat. As he flung himself into the settle again he said, 'I don't know what the devil makes you take such an interest in my affairs.'

Mrs. Veale looked hard at him, and answered, 'A woman can't be indifferent to a goodlooking man.' Charles tossed off his glass to hide his confusion. So this bleached creature had fallen in love with him!—a woman his senior by some fifteen years. He was flattered, but felt that the situation was unpleasant.

'This is a bad world,' he said, 'and I wish I had the re-making of it. The good luck goes to the undeserving.'

'That is only true because those who have wits want readiness. A screw will go in and hold where a nail would split. Coombe Park is yours by right; it has been taken from you by wrong. I should get it back again were I you, and not be too nice about the means.' Charles sighed and shook his head.

'What a life you would lead as young squire,' said Mrs. Veale. 'The maidens now run after Larry Nanspian, because he is heir to Chimsworthy, and don't give much attention to you, because you've nothing in present and nothing in prospect. But if you were at Coombe Park they'd come round you thick as damsels in Shushan to be seen of Ahasuerus, and Larry Nanspian would be nowhere in their thoughts.' She laughed scornfully. 'And the fellows that turn up their noses at you now, because you eat Langford's bread crusts and earn ninepence, how they would cringe to you and call you sir, and run errands for you, and be thankful for a nod or a word! Then the farmers who now call you a good-for-naught would pipe another note, and be proud to shake hands. And Parson Robbins would wait with his white gown on, and not venture to say, "When the wicked man," till he saw you in the Coombe Park pew. And the landlord's door at the "King of Bells" would be ever open to you, and his best seat by the fire would be yours. And I—poor I—would be proud to think I'd poured out a glass of Plymouth spirit to the young squire, and that he'd listened to my foolish words.'

Charles tossed his head, and threw up and turned over the crown in his trousers pocket. Then, unsolicited, he poured himself out another glass and tossed it off. That would be a grand day when he was squire and all Bratton was at his feet.

Mrs. Veale stood erect before him with flickering eyes. 'Do y' know the stone steps beside the door?' she asked.

'Yes!'

'What be they put there for?'

'They are stepping-stones to help to mount into the saddle.'

'What stones be they?'

'I'm sure I can't say,'

'Right; no more does he know or care who uses them. Well, I'm naught, but I can help you into the saddle of Coombe Park.'

CHAPTER XVIII.

TREASURE TROVE.

Charles Luxmore was not able to sleep much that night. It was not that his conscience troubled him. He gave hardly a thought to the affair at the circus. His imagination was excited; that delusive faculty, which, according to Paley, is the parent of so much error and evil. The idea of Coombe Park recurred incessantly to his mind and kept him awake. But it was not the acquisition of wealth and position that made the prospect so alluring; it was the hope of crowing over all those who had despised him, of exciting the envy of those who now looked down on him.

The 'Ring of Bells' was on the Coombe estate. How he could swagger there as the landlord's overlord! The Nanspians, Taverner Langford, had but a few hundred acres, and the Coombe Park property was nigh on two thousand.

Squire Impey and he would be the two great men of the place, and as the squire at Culm Court was a hunting man, he, Charles Luxmore, would be hand in glove with him.

It would be worth much to ride in scarlet after the hounds, with his top boots and a black velvet cap, and the hand holding a whip curled on the thigh so, and to jog past old Langford, and cast him a "Do, Taverner, this morning? Middling, eh?' and to crack the whip at Hillary Nanspian and shout, 'Out o' the way, you cub, or I'll ride you down.' He sat up in bed and flapped his arms, holding the blanket as reins, and clicked with his tongue, and imagined himself galloping over the field after the hounds at full cry. Right along Broadbury, over the fences of Langford, across Taverner's land, tearing, breaking through the hedges of Chimsworthy, tally-ho! With a kick, Charles sent the bedclothes flying on to the floor.

'By George!' he said. 'We shall have a meet in front of Coombe Park, and Honor and Kate shall serve out cherry-brandy to the huntsmen.' Then he scrambled about the floor collecting his bed-clothes and rearranging them. 'I'll go to Coombe Park to-morrow, and look where the kennels are to be. I'll give an eye also to the pond. I don't believe it has been properly cleaned out and fit for trout since the place left our hands. I'm afraid Honor will never rise to her situation—always keep a maid-of-all-work mind. Confound these bed-clothes, I've got them all askew.'

So possessed was Charles with the idea that it did not forsake him when morning came. It clung to him all the day. 'There's only a hundred pounds wanted,' he said, 'for us to establish our claim.'

Then he paused in the work on which he was engaged. 'How am I to reach a hundred pounds on ninepence a day, I'd like to know? Ninepence a day is four-and-six a week, and that makes eleven guineas or thereabouts per annum. I must have something to spend on clothing and amusement. Say I put away seven guineas in the year, why it would take me thirteen to fourteen years to earn a hundred pounds—going straight as a nail, not as a screw, nor as a ferret.'

In the evening Charles wandered away to Coombe Park. The owner, a yeoman named Pengelly, who, however, owned only the home farm, not the entire property, had been accustomed to the visits of Oliver Luxmore, which had been regarded as a sort of necessary nuisance. He was by no means disposed to have his place haunted by the young man also, of whose conduct he had received a bad report from all sides. He therefore treated Charles with scant courtesy, and when young Luxmore tried bluster and brag, he ordered him off the premises.

Charles returned to Langford foaming with rage. Mrs. Veale awaited him.

'The master is not home,' she said; 'where have you been?'

'Been to see my proper home,' he answered, 'and been threatened with the constable if I did not clear away. What do you mean by giving me all sorts of ideas and expectations, and subjecting me to insult, eh? answer me that.'

'Don't you fly out in flaming fury, Mr. Charles.'

'I'm like to when treated as I have been. So would you. So will you, if what I hear is like to come about. There's talk of a hare-hunt.'

'A what?'

'A hare-hunt.'

'Where?' Mrs. Veale stood before him growing deadlier white every moment, and quivering in all her members and in every fibre of her pale dress, in every hair of her blinking eyelids.

'Why here—at Langford.'

She caught his arm and shook him. 'You will not suffer it! You will stay it!'

'Should they try it on, trust me,' said Charles mockingly. 'Specially if Larry Nanspian be in it. I've a grudge against him must be paid off.'

Mrs. Veale passed her hand over her brow. 'To think they should dare!

should dare!' she muttered. 'But you'll not suffer it. A hare-hunt! what do they take me for?'

Charles Luxmore uttered a short ironical laugh. 'Dear blood!'[1] she muttered, and her sharp fingers nipped and played on his arm as though she were fingering a flute. 'You'll revenge me if they do! Trust me! when I'm deadly wronged I can hurt, and hurt I will, and when one does me good I repay it—to a hundred pounds.'

[1] A Devonshire expression, meaning 'Dear fellow.'

She laughed bitterly. There was something painful in her laugh. It was devoid of mirth, and provoked no laughter. Although she said many odd things, invented quaint similes, or used those which were traditional, they hardly ever awoke a smile, her tone was so cheerless, husky and unpleasant.

'So Farmer Pengelly insulted you! Ha! it would be a most laughable conceit to prove that he had no title, and had thrown away his thousands.'

'On Coombe Park?'

'On what else? What did he say to you?'

'Never mind what he said. What he said hurt me. He called me a vagabond and empty pocket, and said I might go pack to the devil.'

'And when you have established your right, and shown that he bought without a proper title, then you'd stand on the doorsteps, stick in hand, and say, Pengelly! who has the empty pocket? Who is the vagabond without a house? Go pack to the devil. What be you to stye in a gentleman's mansion? Whom God Almighty made an ass bides an ass. And cats as ain't got manners must keep off Turkey carpets.'

Then, still holding his arm, she said, 'Come here! I've never shown you over this house; not that Langford is fit to compare with Coombe Park. Yet this were a gentleman's house once. But what were the Langfords as compared with the Luxmores? You'll see a Luxmore monument at the very altar-steps o' the chancel in Bratton Church, but that of a Langford is half-way down the nave, which shows how different they were estimated.' After a short silence, Charles felt a spasmodic quiver pass over her, like the thrill of a peacock when spreading its tail. 'They would have a hare-hunt, would they, and put me to a public shame?'

'No, no, Mrs. Veale,' said Charles caressingly, 'I'll put a stop to that; and if they venture I'll break the necks of those that have to do with it.'

'Come with me,' said the woman hoarsely, 'I'll show you all. Here,' she flung open the sitting-room door, 'here is the parlour where your sister went down on her knees to the master. If he'd ha' axed her to lick his boots she'd ha' done it—no proper pride in her—and all for ninepence a day.'

Charles became very red in the face.

'This is the desk at which the master writes and does his accounts. In it, I reckon, be his books. I've never seed them, and I doubt if I could make much out of 'em if I did. Them things don't agree wi' my faculties, as the cherub said of the armchair.'

'Does old Langford always sit in this room?'

'Oh yes! too proud to sit in the kitchen wi' such as me—not even in winter. Then I must make his fire here every day, and have the worry of keeping it in. There is one thing don't suit him now he is cut wi' the Nanspians. Formerly he got all his fuel from their wood. There are no plantations on Langford, and the old trees are cut down. When he got his fuel at Chimsworthy he hadn't to pay, and now he must get a rick of firing elsewhere.' She pointed to an old-fashioned cupboard in the wall. 'There he keeps his sugar and his tea and his currants. He keeps all under key, lest I or the maidens should steal them. Now you look at me, and I'll show you something.' She opened an empty place under the cupboard and knocked upwards thrice with her fist, and the glass doors of the repository of the groceries flew open. She laughed huskily. 'There! if I strike I shoot up the bolt, and the lock won't hold the doors together. When I press them together and shut back, down falls the bolt.'

'That is ingenious, Mrs. Veale—stay, don't shut yet. I have a sweet tooth, and see some raisins in the bag there.'

'Now leave them alone. I've something better to show you. Men reckon themselves clever, but women beat them in cleverness. Go to the fire-place. Kneel at it, and put your hand up on the left side, thrust in your arm full length and turn the hand round.'

'I shall dirty myself. I shall get a black hand.'

'Of course you will. That is how I found it out. Don't be afraid of a little soot. There is a sort of oven at the side. This room were not always a parlour, I reckon; there were a large open fire-place in it, and when the grate was put in it left the space behind not at all, or only half, filled in—leastways, the road to the oven door was not blocked. Have you found it?'

'Yes,' answered Charles. 'I have my hand in something.'

'And something in your hand, eh?'

'Yes, a box, a largish box.'

He drew forth a tin ease, very heavy, with a handle at the top. It was locked with a letter padlock.

'Into that box the master puts all his savings. I reckon there be hundreds of pounds stowed away there, may be thousands. The master himself don't know how much. He's too afeared of being seen or heard counting it. When he has money he takes out the box, opens it, and puts in the gold, only gold and paper, no silver. Banks break. He will have none of them, but this old cloam oven he thinks is secure. He may be mistaken.'

'How did you find this out?'

'By his black hand. Whenever he had sold bullocks or sheep, and I knew he had received money, so sure was he to come in here with a white hand and come out with one that was black, that is how I found it. I know more. I know the word that will open the box.'

'How did you find that out?'

'The master was himself afraid of forgetting it, and I chanced to see in the first leaf of his Bible here in pencil the reference Gen. xxxvi. 23. One day I chanced to look out the passage, and it was this: "The children of Shobal were these: Alvan, and Manahath, and Ebal, Shepho, and Onam." I thought a man must have a bad conscience to find comfort in such a passage as that. And what do y' think? I found the same reference in his pocket-book. Then I knew it must mean something I didn't see the end of. And one day I were full o' light, like a lantern. I saw it all. Do y' see, this new padlock makes only four letter words, and in that verse there are two words of four letters, and I found as how the master changed about. One year he took Ebal and next year Onam. It be the turn o' Ebal now.'

Charles felt the weight of the case and turned the padlock towards him.

'Lord!' exclaimed Mrs. Veale, 'what if the master have got his thousand or two there! It's nothing to what might be yours if you had Coombe Park.'

Suddenly both started. Langford's voice was heard outside. Charles hastily replaced the case where he had found it, and slipped out of the room with Mrs. Veale, who held him and drew him after her, her nervous fingers playing on his arm-bone as on a pipe.

'Come here,' she whispered, 'let me wash your hand. It is black. Here, at the sink.' She chuckled as she soaped his hand and wrist. 'And here the master have washed his, and thought I did not consider it.' Then she quivered through her whole body and her eyes blinked. She put up her shaking finger, and whispered 'Ebal!'

END OF THE FIRST VOLUME.